Cover design by Kelsi Jerene

Human Authored Reg #: 9799520, https://authorsguild.org/human

www.emmabrattin.com
X: @brattinemma
F: /emmabrattin
I: /emmabrattin

Thank you to the ladies on the plane for naming Harold. Ryan and June for their input on characters and street names. My beautiful hand model. Everybody that shared my name in conversations around the world. My Wichita girls--your advice and encouragement make me who I am. The horse race betting gentlemen on the patio. The humans that dealt with me sitting at tables for hours—please assume I'm talking about you, because there are so many of you that support me at my spots. Everybody that is so excited to be my beta readers. I really can't make a good book without any of you.

CHAPTER ONE

HANNAH

THE MOMENT MY eyes opened, I knew I'd be late.

Again.

I squeezed them shut, chasing the soft whispers of a dream I'd been tossed out of. The feeling of the dream was so close, so fresh, but it wouldn't return. I gave up and opened my eyes. The sun was already high, but a heavy cloud cover muted the daylight to a flat grey.

Here we go again.

One hour later, wearing heeled black boots, a fitted brown skirt, and a purple-and-brown blazer, I descended the stairs from third story to the main exit. Opening the door caused a vacuum effect in the hallway and my brown hair flew into my face.

So glad I curled it today, I thought sarcastically.

The sky was dull and damp as I walked up the sidewalk to Delaware Street where my job awaited. Snow stood in waves against the building edges, and cars rolled by, careful to avoid the crusty potholes that winter and snowplows created. Tucking my blazer closer to my waist, the usual pre-work anxiety wrapped around my throat.

Nobody likes me there. Why do I even go? I'll probably be fired today. I've been late every day this week. Four days in a row was a fireable offense, I'm sure. I'm not even that good. They definitely should fire me.

Maybe then I'd be free.

"Stop it!" I said out loud to myself, startling a dog just about to use a weathered fire hydrant on the sidewalk. The equally weathered owner stared at me confused, and I shrugged. "Not you, sorry."

Twenty-one feels too old to be late to work. But that's tomorrow's problem.

Maybe I'd set my alarm a little earlier for tomorrow. Make myself breakfast.

The shivering set in as I looped a wide berth around the fluffy dog and man and continued to the office building. Wind swirled salt against my ankles and pushed through my skin.

Entering the vestibule should have brought relief, but it didn't. All I felt were more degrading thoughts. I entered the elevator with eleven other suited humans who looked like they did something important. Sweat gathered in my palms. My knees trembled.

This was routine. I did this every day.

Only a few more seconds.

The elevator dinged and four others and I stepped off at six. I breathed a sigh of relief before the next wave crashed into me.

What if someone's already taken over your desk and they just forgot to tell you you've been fired? Maybe you'll be escorted out like Jerry was last month when he threatened the office. Has anybody threatened the office since then? Before? What if he left a bomb that hadn't detonated yet? Did he hate you enough to find you at your house?

"Hannah?" A voice said, startling me from my doomsday panic.

My boss, Debbi, stared over her bifocals, concern pinching her face. Short and heavy, red curls spilled onto her forehead, she hunched over the keyboard, hugging the desk. She'd once told me that if she was ever fired, she'd live under her desk. She'd laughed when she said it. I believed her.

"Hannah, are you okay?" Debbi asked again scrunching her nose to keep the bifocals from slipping further.

"Ah, sorry. Yes. Had an issue at home I had to see to. I promise this isn't going to be the new norm." I ducked my head and walked to my cubicle. At my desk, I buried my face in my hands as if it weighed the same as the building.

I reminded myself I used to love my job. I needed to get my shit together.

Lying to Debbi felt wrong, but I had no real excuse. Couldn't just burst out and say I had severe anxiety coming here since Jerry's drama. Everybody else seemed fine, so I should be, too.

The company had provided safe people to talk to after the event, but I never knew what to say. I'd told the police officers Jerry had always been gentle. Quiet. A little strange, maybe—but kind to me. He loved old card games and talked about collecting them since he was a kid—long before my time. A nerd, like me.

Then he'd shot a gun at work.

The event happened on a Monday. The office shut down the rest of the week for employees to process. Tuesday, I paced my apartment for three hours straight and then proceeded to rip apart four books before I understood what I'd done. Wednesday, I screamed for twenty minutes when I cut my hands slicing an apple. Thursday, I stared at the wall for three hours. Friday, I tripped in the kitchen and punched the cabinet. I later found my cat hiding in a drawer with the pans. After a can of tuna and half an hour of coaxing, she climbed out and settled in my lap. We sat on the floor together for a long time. I tried to cry, to think, to process. Nothing came.

I was numb. And numb felt safer than falling apart. I wanted my job. I would keep showing up.

The following Monday we all showed up and carried on as if nothing had happened. I didn't want to interrupt the flow; we were a productive team. But I didn't feel like I'd moved past anything. How did everybody else?

Lifting my head from my hands, I logged into my computer and began my morning tasks. The dream from this morning kept nudging me. It felt peaceful, as if something good had occurred.

I remember a kid smiling at me. And waves. I heard waves, too. I usually only dreamt about Jerry and the office incident. How he…

Barbara, the mail carrier, dropped a stack of envelopes on my desk making me jump.

Yeah, I need more adrenaline spikes. Thanks.

I rolled my eyes and started sorting the envelopes by priority. A chill went up my spine as I came across a pale-yellow envelope. My hand hovered above it. The handwriting was perfect.

Hannah Ryan

Customs

c/o Janeris International

157 Delaware Ave

Buffalo, NY 13303

No, dear God, this can't be. No, no, no.

The office din swelled into a roar. My breathing quickened. I'd recognize that handwriting anywhere – it belonged to Jerry. Jerry and I worked closely. He was obsessed with sticky notes. There were sticky notes on his computer, his chair, his cubicle walls--even on the men's bathroom mirror. He'd been complimented for his perfect handwriting, which he called a scrawl.

Nausea climbed into my throat and sweat spread across my low back.

What does he want? I can't open this! Should I call the police? Isn't he in jail? Is he coming for me again?!

The envelope laughed at me. The ink lifted off the pages and stung my eyes.

I sobbed, choking breaths broken between murmured fragments. I glanced over at Debbi who was on the phone gossiping about something. I turned my head and leaned back, trying to look into Harold's office, but his door was closed.

Jerry isn't finished here. He'll come back and finish us off.

I didn't know who to tell about the envelope. If I told Debbi, she'd gossip. Harold was followed closely by the office security, Mr. Leota, and I didn't need attention on my poor attendance.

I jumped from my chair and ran to the window. Staring down at the intersection of West Huron Street and Delaware Avenue, I pried my thoughts away from the envelope.

Breathe, Hannah! You can't come undone in front of everybody! Calm yourself down before telling. The therapist said to focus on what was right in front of me.

What do I see?

The sun tried to break through the heavy clouds, casting an eerie glow on the intersection below. Blowing leaves raced through the streets, gathering in corners and drains. A young boy walked hesitantly down Delaware Street facing Huron Street Deli.

"I like their bear claws and iced tea," I said in a whisper. "The lady that works there is a witch, but her husband is a sweet man."

My body let go—my heart slowed, the tightness inside me softened.

Yes, Hannah! I coached myself. *What else do you see?*

I watched the boy approach the deli window and put both his hands against his head to see through the reflective glass window. Just as quickly, he jumped back and looked at the ground. His shoulders slumped forward as he faced the street.

Guess it's the witch today.

"I'll go there for a snack and get the kid something, too," I mumbled to myself as I glanced at my sweaty hands. "I need fresh air anyway."

CHAPTER TWO

LINCOLN

MOM SLEPT IN again. She sleeps a lot. She's been sick as long as I can remember. Ms. Ruber, my principal, said if I was late for school anymore, I'd probably fail second grade. I'm good at finding my way to school, but sometimes I still get lost. I don't want to fail second grade. That would be embarrassing. Who fails second grade?

A lady from a nearby church used to drive me, but her family moved to Springville. I should probably learn how the bus works because I hear other kids can take it for free. I don't know who to ask about that. It's probably not free anyway. Nothing is free, my mom says.

I pulled on yesterday's jeans and the blue hoodie I wear most days. The sleeve was torn by the elbow and my thumb got stuck. The cereal box was empty, but I licked a few crumbs from the bottom of the bag. I peeked into Mom's room. The room smelled like medicine and something sour. I told her I was leaving, even though I knew she wouldn't answer.

On my way to school, I decided to stop by Huron Street Deli, just in case. I was hungry. Hungrier than most mornings.

If Mr. Irving was working, he'd have a sack breakfast ready for me. If his wife was there, she'd shoo me off. I call her the Deli Devil because she is one. I've heard her real name, but I don't like to say it. She doesn't like kids. Maybe she likes some kids, because I heard her husband talk about his daughter once. But she doesn't like me.

My stomach growled. I pressed my hands against the glass to block the reflection, hoping to see Mr. Irving.

Nope.

Deli Devil.

I moved away from the window quickly as she turned to look at me. Guess I'll eat after school. Maybe Mom will get out of bed and go to the store. Or maybe that nice church lady next door will drop something off. Sometimes the lunch lady leaves me food, too.

Don't cry, Lincoln, I reminded myself.

My stomach twisted.

I didn't sleep well last night. Mom made a lot of noises. I think her medicine is running low. She cries out in her sleep and runs to the bathroom when that happens. I bring her a cold washcloth most times and drape it across the back of her neck. She always looks at me so sad that I wonder if I make her sickness worse, but then she squeezes my hands and asks me to leave. I like when she squeezes my hands back. I know she's telling me it's okay.

I think she'll be better soon. She has to be. I'm sure her medicine will help.

My stomach hurt and I glanced back at the deli. Deli Devil stood at the door with her arms crossed. She looked angry. Like I'd stolen from her. My chest tightened as if I'd actually done something bad.

I didn't take anything from you. Why do you hate me? I wanted to yell at her.

I felt like crying, but Mom used to say I was too old for tears. Crying was for babies. She said I had to be a man and take care of her.

I heard honking and froze. I hadn't been paying attention.

Suddenly the street didn't look familiar, and I didn't know which way to turn.

A car screeched. Another swerved toward me.

I ran for the sidewalk.

Metal crunched. Something scraped.

It was so loud I covered my ears.

I wish Mom would just get better.

I'm scared.

Alone.

I'm hungry.

I wish someone would come.

I have no idea where I am.

I didn't feel like a man anymore.

I fell to the ground and cried anyway.

CHAPTER THREE

HANNAH

I FOCUSED ON one thing: get a snack. The elevator door shut. Pressure lifted off my shoulders.

One moment at a time.

Exiting the building, I glanced towards the deli, looking for the kid. I stepped off the front door stoop and heard the grotesque crunch of metal.

I whipped around to my left as a large black vehicle shoved a smaller car into a light pole at the intersection.

My breath caught as the little kid I saw from my office window ran from the middle of the street.

He jumped onto the sidewalk and collapsed by my feet.

The world quieted, as if someone had turned down the volume.

I crouched down and put my hand on the kid's back.

"Hi, buddy. Are you okay?" I said softly.

The dirty blonde boy, around eight, glanced up and I caught his eye. Tears on his cheeks caught the light snowflakes swirling around us. He was shaking. I wasn't.

He stared at me with large blue eyes for a moment, like he was searching for something. He felt familiar in a way I couldn't explain.

People started shouting and we both looked up as tires squealed.

I gathered the kid against me as the SUV reversed from the sedan and made a U-turn, heading toward the skyway.

Where the hell are you going?!

Sirens echoed. For a moment, I couldn't tell which way was forward. The air smelled like hot metal, and I knew something irreversible had just happened.

The kid put his arms around me and squeezed briefly. Then he slipped away and ran down the sidewalk. The place he'd stood against me was suddenly cold.

"Wait! Hey!" I yelled after him, reaching out. He kept going and buried himself in the crowd.

"Someone help!" A woman's voice yelled.

The woman was pointing to the sedan.

Where are the first responders?

Without thinking, I started jogging to the sedan. Another man joined me and we attempted to pry open the crumpled passenger door.

"Where is the other vehicle?" The woman yelled.

I looked down at the ground.

No skid marks. The SUV never even braked. Wonder if he was having a heart attack then woke up and realized what'd happened? But then, why did he leave?

"I got it!" The man helping me yelled and swung open the passenger door.

"Good work!" I responded. "I'll check on him!"

I ducked inside the car and saw a late-twenties man slumped over the steering wheel. Blood dripped off his temple onto the seat.

"Sir? Sir, we need to get you out of this car," I said as I shook his shoulder.

His body shifted at my touch, but he didn't wake.

"Sir? Can you hear me?"

I felt hands grab my waist. I slapped one away and looked behind me.

Paramedics.

"Sorry," I mumbled as I stepped out of their way.

A firefighter started unrolling the hose on the side of his truck. The sedan was smoking heavily.

The paramedics pulled the man out from the passenger side and laid him on a stretcher. The firefighters started yelling and the paramedics ran back to the car, away from the man.

I walked over to him. Dark curls spilled across his forehead, mixed with blood and sweat. Long eyelashes fluttered.

I leaned forward to move his hair off his forehead when he grabbed my hand. I glanced up to meet green eyes staring at me like I was the ghost.

“Find him,” he breathed, his hand warm on mine. “Protect him. I’ll be there as soon as I can.”

He gulped in air. His eyes closed. He dropped my hand as the paramedics returned, and once again I was asked to step back. I stumbled backwards enough for the gurney to pass by.

I heard a voice trying to get my attention and turned around.

“Ma’am? Hi, sorry. Did you witness the accident?”

I recognized a female field reporter from Channel 6, our local new station.

“I’m Shelia Temprua, Channel 6 News. Can you tell me what you observed in this particular incident?”

The reporter’s monotone voice grated my nerves, but I complied with a short nod.

What did I even just see? Where is the boy?

She held a microphone up to my lips. I stared at the fuzzy edges, unable to focus.

Where is he?

I looked around me, searching the crowd.

"Ma'am?"

"Uh, yes, sorry. I've seen accidents from the window before," I told the short reporter as she held the microphone in my face. I pointed up at my office building looming over my head. "I work on the sixth floor. My desk looks right over this intersection. But I've never been right next to it."

"Can you tell me what you saw?"

"Sure, I guess. A kid ran into the street, against the light, but a sedan moved into the intersection blocking an SUV from hitting him," I said, summarizing what I'd witnessed.

"The sedan's quick movement saved that kid?" Shelia interrupted.

"Yeah, yeah, I suppose he did. The kid ran to the sidewalk and just fell down sobbing. Little guy, too. Wonder where his parents are? I hope he's okay. Has anybody seen him?" I stopped and glanced at the cameraman who shrugged. I shivered.

"Thank you," the reporter said to me somberly. She turned to the camera. "What a thing to witness—a daring sacrifice. From Delaware Avenue, Buffalo, I'm Shelia Temprua. Channel 6 News."

The cameraman put his camera down and another woman approached me asking for my name. I probably shouldn't have given her my name, but I kept replaying the moment the boy's eyes caught mine, my chest tight each time. I swear I heard ocean waves.

My teeth started chattering and I wondered if the boy was still shaking.

Who is taking care of him?

A police officer approached me and asked if I'd write a statement. I glanced at the deli and yearned for my snack and my office chair but complied. I described the SUV best I could and recounted what I'd told the reporter.

Who thought I'd want to be at my desk on purpose.

CHAPTER FOUR

LINCOLN

THE LADY WITH the curly hair and another man were so brave trying to open that beat-up car. I couldn't believe I ran into the street like that. I knew better! And I caused someone else to get hurt because of my stupid baby tears.

I'm glad to see the emergency people get that guy out of his car. He looked knocked out or something until he grabbed that lady's arm. She nearly jumped as high as the building. He said something to her then passed back out. I wondered if he was asking who I was so he could yell at me for letting him get hurt. I hope he wakes up. I should probably find him and apologize.

Where did ambulances take sick people around here?

I slipped back into the crowd and tried to act casual.

"Uh, sir, where does the ambulance go in this town?"

The man didn't even glance down, but he mumbled something about Buff-Gen.

I figured that meant Buffalo General Hospital.

I'd been there with Mom before. I could go there after school. I wouldn't mind going right now, but I needed to get food. I hoped Miss Maggie would have food for me today. Mom hadn't eaten in a couple days. I was lucky to have a lunch lady like her.

The lady from the sidewalk didn't push me away. She was warm. Like when Mom squeezes my hand. For a second, I felt like I wasn't alone.

I thought about Mom lying in bed.

Mom is a good mom. She's just really sick. It's not her fault.

My throat felt tight.

School.

Hospital.

Feed mom.

I looked around and focused on where I was.

With a plan in my head, I felt better. I headed toward the elementary school.

CHAPTER FIVE

HANNAH

AFTER THE OFFICER ran out of questions, I asked if I could go back to work. He nodded and closed his writing pad. I glanced up at the sixth floor and decided I'd still get a snack at the deli before going back.

Not my fault I'll be late coming back from break this time.

Crossing was easy. The intersection was still closed. I dodged an oncoming tow truck and stepped into the deli. A holiday bell jingled as the door closed behind me.

A lady with a long nose and low bun asked what I'd like. I ordered a pastry with cream cheese filling and hot tea.

She turned to pour the water as a man sitting behind the glass case stood up. I jumped a little because I didn't realize he was back there.

"Is the boy in the street okay?" He asked gruffly.

I didn't answer at first. The woman snorted loudly. I glanced over at her then back at the man.

"He didn't get hit, but I don't know where he is now. Do you know him?"

I stepped closer to the counter and put both hands on the glass, deciding to ignore the woman's reaction.

"He's..." the man began.

"Irving, mind your business," she said, tossing her head in my direction. "Ma'am, we're not the Yellow Pages, and even if we were, that's not our business."

"Rhonda..."

"Irving, I hear the timer in the back. Pack up this order then go get the macaroons out of the oven before they burn."

Irving put his hands on his knees and stood up. He dipped his head towards the woman then pulled on clear gloves and began wrapping my order.

I watched her as she huffed at the man then walked around the glass cabinet to straighten some tea leaf boxes that were slightly askew.

The man seemed gentle to me, but they clearly had history. Married a long time, maybe.

I smelled Earl Grey tea as the man reached out two hands towards me. I tried to grab the brown paper sack from his hand, but I felt resistance. I glanced up and his eyes met mine–as if he wanted to say more–then he released the tea and sack.

Irving's expression stayed with me as I left the deli. I was at my desk before I realized I was back at work.

I set the paper sack on the desk and flipped back the lid, breathing in the acidic fragrance. My hands were still shaking from the adrenaline rush, but not enough to slosh hot water over the sides. I felt impressed with myself. Or maybe I still hadn't processed what I'd just been through.

Who knows what that will do to me.

I recalled ripping books and shoved the thought aside. I reached for the pastry. The paper bag shifted and I felt cold again.

The envelope.

I looked at the pale-yellow envelope and Jerry's perfect handwriting.

My name. He wrote my *name.*

I shoved the brown sack over the envelope and looked up at the ceiling.

"Has the mail come yet?" Harold's voice startled me and I glanced down at the envelope. I looked over at Harold, tapping on his smartwatch with quick, irritated jabs.

"Yes, sir," I said. "Sorry for the delay—I witnessed an accident downstairs. A little boy..."

"Yeah, crazy accident," Debbi cut in with her usual cheerful tone, hovering just behind Harold.

She caught my eye and mouthed no.

Harold glanced behind him at Debbi who smiled at him. He glanced back at me with his eyebrows scrunched together in a question. Debbi's silent warning echoed in my ears and the envelope waited beneath the bag. I needed to stop this conversation right away.

"I'll work on it right now, sir." I matched Debbi's smile and turned toward my desk.

Harold opened his mouth, then paused and stepped closer.

"Sir, your call with Singapore branch is in two minutes," Debbi said. "Please head to the conference room now."

Harold stopped and looked at his watch again. He rolled his eyes and started pressing buttons on the tiny screen.

"Right," he replied, distracted from whatever he'd had on his mind.

Debbi cast a worried look my direction, then her smile resurfaced as she shooed Harold towards the conference room.

She waited for him to walk away then said, "I can't afford for this place to implode, Hannah." She nodded and followed Harold down the hall.

Why can't I talk about the accident? Debbi, the office gossip, knows everything. Perhaps she knows where I can find that boy.

I felt someone watching me.

Mr. Leota.

I nodded at the security guy as he stomped past my desk, his gaze sharp and lingering.

What a brute. He annoys me more than he scares me. Somehow that feels worse.

I watched him walk away, then slid the envelope into my purse. It felt heavier than paper should. Everything tilted out of place.

I wasn't opening it here — not with everyone watching, not with Jerry's name still churning in my head. I hadn't even decided if it was mine to open.

His voice came back to me.

Protect him.

How could I protect someone I didn't even know? A kid, at that.

My stomach growled and I shoved my hand into the paper sack. Quickly unwrapping the pastry, I took a bite of cream cheese and sugar. I focused on eating. My hands settled. I remembered that tomorrow I'd be twenty-one. The thought passed me without celebration, like a fact I hadn't agreed to yet.

Maybe I should make plans with someone. Or do something. Pretend that every moment doesn't make me jump and every thought doesn't make me sweat.

Pastry gone, I began to crumble the wrapper when my stomach dropped. I carefully flattened the wrapper on top of the desk. Written across the bottom in quick, uneven strokes:

4176 N WOODROW

CHAPTER SIX

LINCOLN

BY THE TIME the second bell rang, I had been in trouble three times. My ears were hot, and I stared at the floor.

The first time was for being late. I completely missed first period. I promised it wouldn't happen tomorrow, even though I wasn't sure. I wanted it to be true.

Next, I was sent to the principal's office because Miss Dawson said I wasn't paying attention and made a fool of her during third hour.

I kept thinking about that woman from the sidewalk.

So, I guess she was right.

Finally, I tripped in P.E. and knocked over two other kids, who happened to be smaller than me. Mr. Burns told me he was putting a demerit on my record — wherever that is.

After gym I went to my locker to get books for my next class and passed the lunch lady, Miss Maggie. She nodded at me and I forgot all the trouble for a moment. When she did that, it meant I could take home leftovers from lunch.

Mom will eat today.

I try to bring food to Mom whenever I can. She's been sick for a long time. She doesn't really get out of bed at all. She mumbles and itches. Sometimes the church ladies will bring food by, but I haven't seen them in a couple weeks.

I saw on T.V. that shingles is pretty common for old people and that it hurts and itches really bad. That's probably what she has.

I wonder if the hospital has any medicine for moms with shingles.

I remembered the people at the accident talking about taking that man to

Buff-Gen Hospital. Maybe I could tell him I was sorry and get Mom help, too.

One period before lunch, I went back to my locker. My stomach rumbled and I hoped it was pizza day.

A small scrap of paper sat inside the door. It read:

11:00 AM

I looked at the clock above my locker. The red numbers said 10:55 AM. Miss Maggie usually told me to come by at 1:30. Something must have changed.

I ran to the lunchroom and found a sack of food on the table inside the door. I grabbed it and decided I wasn't going back to class. It had been a bad day. Tomorrow would be better.

Today I was going to find the man and get medicine for Mom at the hospital.

And I wanted to find the curly-haired woman.

I grabbed my backpack and snuck out of school.

I headed toward downtown.

CHAPTER SEVEN

HANNAH

I STARTED SORTING the remaining mail, trying hard not to think about the address. My phone danced across the desk. I picked it up to find a text from my best friend, Lucy.

WHAT ARE WE DOING TOMORROW???...SHOTS!!

I rolled my eyes.

Like I'd do shots.

But I was happy that someone else was thinking about my birthday.

Before I could stop myself, I typed:

CAN YOU PICK ME UP IN FIVE AT WORK? NEED TO CHECK OUT AN ADDRESS.

I saw three blue dots pop up then disappear and I instantly felt silly. Why was I doing this? What was I going to do if I found the kid? Kidnap him?

I long pressed on the message, intending to delete, when Lucy's reply popped up.

HOPEFULLY WE'RE STALKING A NEW BOYFRIEND. ALTHOUGH BEN DOESN'T APPROVE. AT DORM.
WILL PICK YOU UP IN FIVE.

I smiled. Everything I loved about Lucy was right there.

She doesn't ask questions, she just shows up.

With Lucy and Ben, I didn't have to explain why my hands shook after a sudden noise. We'd learned each other's tells a long time ago.

I carefully folded the wrapper and filed it in my purse near the envelope. Standing up, I slid a coat over my shoulders and reached for my scarf as Mr. Leota approached my cubicle.

"Uh, hi?" I said, frozen with my hand still in the air, and my scarf slowly sliding off my neck.

What is with this guy? He's supposed to be a security guard.

Mr. Leota was a large man, probably twice my size. I'd overheard Debbi say he was likely Samoan. Dark, cropped hair. His neck and shoulders looked like one solid block. Not a man I'd want to cross. He'd been brought in after Jerry's event to protect the employees.

"Where are you going?" Mr. Leota asked, his voice a hollow echo I felt vibrate through my bones.

"What do you care?" I said, adjusting the scarf around my neck. I didn't want him to know he'd rattled me simply by existing.

Mr. Leota grunted and walked over to my desk. I stepped back, bumping into the cubicle wall.

"Harold is waiting for his mail," Mr. Leota reminded.

"I know that, thank you. I will make sure it's done on time. Please leave my stuff alone! What are you doing?"

Mr. Leota began to move items around on my desk, flipping through the stacks of mail near my monitor.

I took a deep breath; glad I had my purse crossed around my body.

Time to get this creep out of my space.

"Mr. Leota, you're a security guard, why are you here on Harold's behalf?"

Probably the wrong thing to say, I yelled at myself as Mr. Leota straightened up to his six-foot-plus height. He turned away from my desk and stepped closer.

Sneering down at me, he said softly, "Of course, my mistake."

His breath smelled of beer and tobacco. He held my gaze for another second, smiling, then sidestepped around me and walked to the conference room.

I gulped air and wondered why I'd provoked him.

What the hell, Hannah. He could snap you in half.

Then a worse thought flooded my veins, and I flushed under my scarf.

They know about the envelope.

My phone vibrated to alert me that Lucy was at the door.

I walked to the elevator and tapped my foot until the doors opened. Exiting the building I saw Ben's bright blue Honda Civic. Lucy rolled down the window and waved me into the back seat. I shut the door of the car, then glanced behind me as Mr. Leota stepped out of the front door. He crossed his arms as he watched us drive away.

Lucy followed my line of sight.

“Who is the guy?” She asked.

“That’s our security guard,” I said, turning around and buckling. I handed the address to Ben in the driver’s seat.

“He’s intense, but I’d date him,” Lucy said with a shrug.

“Gross, Lucy. He’s way older than you,” Ben interjected as he pulled away from the curb and headed north towards Niagara Falls.

“Yeah, but I bet he drives better than you, old man,” Lucy said.

Despite the drama of the day, I couldn’t help but laugh at the sibling banter.

"That reminds me, Hannah, want to go to King's Court tomorrow with me? Your first legal entry to the *real* bars."

I wished I had a real excuse to say no.

"Hey, I can't go there!" Lucy said with a pout, saving me from declining. "I'm only nineteen! And Hannah already said she'd go somewhere with me."

"I did, she's right. I'm sorry, Ben." I said, relieved.

I saw his eyes look for mine in the rearview mirror. He probably knew I was lying.

"How about a double date where the young'ins can go?" I suggested, feeling guilty.

I saw Ben smile at the small win.

I told myself it wouldn't hurt to go out with friends on my birthday.

Lucy started considering which of her guy friends she'd invite.

I looked out the window at a derelict neighborhood.

"We're here," Ben said. "4176 N Woodrow."

He eased the car to a stop along a cracked curb.

At the end of a broken path, a sagging bungalow slouched behind a dilapidated porch. Snow clung to the foundation. I felt cold and wondered how a child could live here.

I didn't know what I expected, but this wasn't it.

CHAPTER EIGHT

HANNAH

BEN PULLED THE car against the curb, but nobody moved. He glanced at me in the rearview mirror with a questioning look.

"Lucy, did you lie to me about what we're doing here?" Ben said.

Lucy didn't even try to deny it.

“I said Hannah needed help.” She shrugged.

Ben exhaled loudly and turned in his seat to face us. His expression wasn’t angry, just worried.

“So, Hannah,” Ben said quietly, “want to explain?”

I hadn’t thought about what I’d say and the silence stretched. Every sentence sounded worse than the reality — that I was following one step at a time.

“I don’t really know how to explain,” I finally mumbled. “I watched a kid almost get hit by a car today. Like, almost die. Someone drove in front of him to stop the oncoming SUV and got t-boned.

Lucy's jaw dropped open and Ben's lips tightened.

"Later," I added, too fast now, "I'm sitting there eating a pastry when I find an address written across it. I know this sounds insane. Hell, it *is* insane. But I feel like I have to do this."

"Find the kid? You think the address is where the kid lives?" Lucy asked, looking out the window at the house.

"Why would *you* need to find the kid, Hannah?" Ben said.

"After we got the driver out of the car, he sort of...woke up. He grabbed my hand and told me to find the kid and protect him."

"What! Your day has been way more exciting than mine!" Lucy said. "Ben, give me that paper with the address on it and I'll do some digging."

"I won't stop you, Hannah, but this whole thing sounds dangerous."

"Ben. Address." Lucy snapped her fingers while retrieving a tablet from her bag.

Ben stared at me for a few more moments, like he was waiting for me to agree with him. When he realized I wouldn't change my mind, he leaned back in his seat, jaw tight.

"Fine, but I'm walking up to the door with you."

He handed Lucy the address and she started tapping her screen.

"Thank you for your concern, Ben, but I'm fine. I can do it alone."

I pulled my shoulders back, pretending confidence. I didn't know why I couldn't just let him come with me.

The concrete walkway was cracked and sinking. Dry grass swirled around my feet as if nobody had walked this stretch of land in years. Lifting my foot onto the first step, I tested the strength of the rotting wood.

I bet this house was cute back in its day.

Confident the porch wouldn't cave in under my weight, I rapped my knuckles on the faded blue door.

I didn't hear anything from inside.

Maybe everybody is right, and this really is nothing. I don't know what to do next.

What the heck am I doing?

Did I put us in danger?

I heard Ben walking up behind me. He didn't say anything and stopped at the bottom of the steps.

"Ben, what are you doing?" I said, turning around.

"It's not a good area, Hannah. Just want to make sure you're safe," Ben replied, putting his hands in his pockets.

A mix of gratitude and irritation hung on my shoulders. I shrugged it off and decided I was glad he was there.

I'm already here. Let's do this.

I faced the door and knocked again. Louder this time.

The door cracked open, then swung wider.

The woman in front of us looked like she'd been interrupted mid-thought—clothes rumpled, skin sallow, eyes rimmed red, as if sleep were optional in her life. Her gaze slid from me to Ben and hardened, defensive but curious.

"Mormons, damn Mormons," she snapped. "I've found God and I don't want cookies. Leave me alone!"

The woman stepped back to shut the door. I put my hand against the door.

"No, please. I'm looking for your son," I said, stepping forward.

I really hope this is the right place.

I heard Ben step up on the first stair.

The frail woman looked me up and down, her eyes twitching, unfocused. She didn't frighten me. She made me feel responsible in a way I didn't understand — like seeing something broken and wishing I could fix it.

I looked beyond her shaggy clothing and saw a dusty hallway with no photographs, no furniture, no sign of life.

No way a kid lives here. Nobody should.

"He's fed, he's fine," the woman replied, softer this time, as if spoken a thousand times.

I nodded like I believed her.

"I just..."

"You can't have him," she said, the words tumbling. Her grip tightened on the door frame.

"No, ma'am," I replied. "I don't want to take your son."

The woman's mouth dropped open slightly and her gaze caught something above my head, like she was watching something only she could see.

"Uh, ma'am?" I said hesitantly.

After a few moments the woman's eyes slid back down to me and she licked her lips.

"Do I look like a nanny? He's in school, moron."

Duh. It's school hours. I kicked myself for not considering that tiny detail.

"Of course. I didn't think of that, so sorry. I can come back later. What time would be better?"

"Don't come back. Lincoln wants nothing to do with you."

"But ma'am..."

Ben tugged firmly on my hand as the front door slammed and a rush of air threw my hair back.

Lincoln.

Protect him.

CHAPTER NINE

HANNAH

I WALKED BACK to the car. I didn't realize Ben was still holding my hand until he opened the door for me.

I gave him a sad, tired look, and pulled my hand away.

Why doesn't Lincoln want anything to do with me? What did he tell his mother?

“He probably hasn’t even been home since the accident, Hannah. Don’t take what she said as truth,” Ben said as if replying to my thoughts. He brushed my hair back gently.

I half smiled and slid into the back seat. As Ben pulled away from the curb, the neighborhood blurred past the window, and my chest tightened for no reason I could explain. The thought of the office—its carpet, the hum of the lights, Harold’s voice, Mr. Leota’s stare—pressed on me. The way I looked at Lincoln’s mom is probably how everyone has looked at me since Jerry shot his gun.

I rolled my shoulders once, then again, like I could force the images away.

Lucy put her hand on my arm and squeezed. I focused on the pressure to ground myself.

"Janeris Trust owns this house," Lucy said, looking me in the eye then back at her brother. She squeezed my arm one more time then dropped her hand. "They've been buying up properties in Niagara Falls to build condos, but some owners won't sell. So the ones they've already bought just sit there and fall into disrepair."

"Janeris Trust? Like Janeris International? The company I work for?" I said.

"It seems that way, yeah," Lucy responded with a shrug. "But what is weird is the house we're at isn't anywhere near the planned condos...it is just a one-off."

"Is Janeris a popular name around here? Could it be a different group?" Ben interjected.

Ben—never afraid to question something, always trying to fix things before they become a problem.

"I suppose," Lucy said, annoyed at being questioned. "I haven't found solid proof that Janeris Trust and Janeris International are one and the same."

I crossed my ankles and leaned back in my seat trying to hear what Lucy was saying. I was fighting away images of the woman clinging to the door frame, and

Lincoln falling fearfully at my feet. I knocked my purse over and bent to gather the dumped contents.

My hand touched the envelope, and I recoiled as if I'd just grabbed a hot coal.

I'd forgotten about the envelope. Perhaps intentionally.

"Uh, guys, there's more," I said hesitantly picking up the envelope. "Remember Jerry and what happened at the office?"

"Uh-oh, what?" Lucy said, her eyes bright.

Ben glanced in the rearview mirror and the car slowed in his distraction.

"Dude, keep driving," Lucy said rolling her eyes at her brother.

"I am! Where am I going?" Ben responded.

"Possibly the police station?" I said.

"Hannah!" Ben said as he began to slow down again.

"I got a letter in the mail at work from Jerry, but I haven't opened it yet. It's addressed to me, but..." I trailed off, unsure if anything made sense anymore.

Lucy snatched the envelope from my lap and considered the handwriting. She held it up to the daylight then handed it back to me.

"It looks like just a piece of paper," Lucy decided. "Probably nothing dangerous."

"I could open it for you, Hannah," Ben said confidently. "Anthrax isn't very popular these days. I'll be careful."

Lucy snickered at her brother's chivalrous offer but agreed with the decision and made an offhanded comment of not wasting a cop's time.

Despite what Jerry had done — and my fear after — I didn't think the contents would be dangerous.

"How about Delaware Park? The police station is close in case something bad is in there," I suggested.

Ben expertly parallel parked in front of a statue on the west end of the park. A few joggers passed, their breath clouds of steam. We slowly climbed out of the car.

"If something does go wrong, nobody else will notice, that's for sure," Lucy said as she observed the mostly empty park.

I handed Ben the envelope and grabbed Lucy's arm. She put her hand on me and we both stepped back.

Ben held the envelope away from him and slowly peeled the glued flap open. He pulled out a single folded sheet of paper.

"In all caps, it says MONSTERS IN YOUR POCKET," Ben said.

"Monsters in your pocket?" Lucy echoed incredulously.

"What do we do with that?" Ben said. "Why is Jerry sending you riddles?"

I didn't understand the words. But I understood this: Jerry hadn't written them for the police. He'd written them for me.

I folded the paper once, then again, until the words disappeared.

"I need to get back to work," I said, though every part of me screamed to stay away.

"Hannah..." Ben said walking closer to me.

"No, it's okay, really. I just need a minute. And I really don't want to get fired."

"Come on, Ben," Lucy said walking towards the car.

The office was waiting. I didn't tell Ben where I was really headed—because if I said it out loud, he'd stop me, or I'd be forced to admit how bad my plan was.

I wasn't going back to sort mail or pretend I was fine.

I was going back because I was tired of being afraid.

CHAPTER TEN

LINCOLN

IT'S BEEN A few months since I've been in this hospital. Last time I was here, Mom had some sort of treatment that made her smile for a couple of days after she came back. She had asked me to sit with her at home that first night. She asked about my school and if I had friends. I didn't tell her I hadn't slept or eaten in two days, but instead pretended I had lots of friends and had just stayed with them while she was away. She'd smiled at me and squeezed my hand, then sent me to bed.

I don't think they gave her the right medicines, though, because she got sick again the next day.

I stood outside the hospital until I saw an adult walk by, then I tagged along with them like I was part of a family. The security guard didn't even glance up when the automatic doors slid open. The smell of the hospital hit me and I wanted to spit, but I pretended I belonged here.

Last time I was here, the nurses told me to sit in a special room on the fifth floor to wait for information on my mom. I went directly there because I knew the nurses stood close by and gossiped. I wasn't going to find this man without help, but when I asked questions, adults asked even more. I didn't need the attention today.

I found the special room again and went directly to the snack bowl. I grabbed a bag of Cheetos and ripped open the bag. Crunching chips nearly drowned out the voices, but I caught a nurse saying something about a handsome stranger with no immediate family. I overheard pieces — car accident, driver fleeing the scene (whatever that meant), victim not doing well. They were waiting for Eiden's test results.

Eiden. Got it.

I wasn't getting any more information from these two nurses because they started babbling about vending machines and the maternity ward being crowded.

I snagged a blue and red bag of chips and tiptoed past the two women and headed toward the elevators.

I'll find another area to wait and listen. I need to figure out where Eiden is.

As I turned the corner to the hallway by the elevators, I saw a nurse typing on a computer on wheels. She glanced up at me and I knew I'd been caught.

Her eyes stayed on me. Not just noticing. Studying.

I'm going to get kicked out or arrested.

She moved away from her computer and took a step toward me.

I looked around for any possible exit, but I knew running would look worse than just staying put. I wasn't a criminal.

My hands went stiff and I almost dropped my chips.

She stopped. Reaching into her pocket, she pulled out a plastic rectangle. With one more glance at me, she turned and hurried in the opposite direction.

As she disappeared around the corner, I let out a deep breath.

I looked at the screen she'd been staring at and opened the second bag of chips. Careful to hold the bag tight, I tossed a chip in my mouth and bit down.

That looks like a list of people in the hospital.

I glanced behind me and in front of me. In the distance I heard squeaky shoes and a few rooms away, a TV yelled at its occupant. I didn't see anybody.

I stepped closer and scanned the names. None of them looked right until I crossed EIDEN KELLY – ROOM 302. I figured that name could be pronounced like I heard the nurses say it, but I'd have spelled it E-D-E-N.

"Son, are you okay?" A voice behind me said.

I jumped and turned around. Instinctively, I shoved another chip in my mouth and mumbled something that even I couldn't understand.

"What's that? Are you lost?" The nurse from before put her arm around my shoulder. She looked down at me. I felt like I was wasting her time—but also liked that she cared enough to ask. Sort of.

"Uh, no, I'm not lost. Um," I had to think fast. I didn't want to go to jail for sneaking in. "My mom is in the maternity ward and asked for the blue cheese-flavored chips. I told her I'd find them.

But I can't. Do you know where they are?" I blinked hard and widened my eyes like kids do on TV.

"Aww, sweetheart, you're absolutely adorable! What floor is your momma on?"

I worked hard to remember what I'd heard the nurses talking about earlier.

"Uhhhh... fifth!"

If I hadn't been so focused on the chips, I'd remember.

Then, it hit me.

"No, fourth! Fourth. And the chips...second floor. I remember she told me where to find them, I just forgot. Mom will be worried if I don't get back soon, ma'am. Will you excuse me?" I smashed another chip in my mouth and mumbled a sort of goodbye.

The nurse opened her mouth to speak then stopped and grabbed her plastic block again.

I didn't wait to see if she believed me. I decided the stairs were my escape and bolted into the stairwell. I rushed down to floor three and shoved open the door into a busy hallway with nurses and doctors and other people rushing about.

I ducked my head and walked toward where I thought Room 302 might be. Trying to catch my breath, I finished my chips and tossed the bag in a trash can in a passing cleaning cart.

I found Room 302 and paused outside the open door.

Earlier, the notes next to Eiden's name in the computer said he wasn't doing well. I began to imagine all the things I might see and wondered why I was here.

You're here to say you're sorry so he isn't mad at you anymore.

A nurse shuffled by from inside the room and I knew it was time to go in. I took another deep breath and stepped inside.

The man from the intersection was sleeping, and there were some cuts on his face.

The beeping in the room grew louder as I walked closer to the bed.

I was close to the top of the bed and glanced back to the door, hoping nobody came in. I looked at the man's feet and considered if I should say something or not since he was sleeping.

"Lincoln?"

I froze.

Eiden's eyes were bright. He didn't look sick at all.

His hand stretched toward me, wires tugging against his wrist.

He's talking to me.

He knows my name!

I jumped away from the bed and ran to the door, not looking back.

"Lincoln, come back!" he yelled.

His voice chased me down the hallway. For a second, something about it tugged at me — like I'd heard it before.

I just want to be home. I need Mom to tell me why this man knows my name.

I ran through the hallway and down the stairway to the ground floor. I slowed as I passed the security guard. The television was blaring and I stopped cold when I heard the reporter say "what a thing to witness—a daring sacrifice. From Delaware Avenue." I looked at the TV above the guard's station.

The images showed the curly-haired woman pulling at the damaged door of the car the man was stuck in after the accident.

She was so brave. I wish I could be brave like her.

The reporter said, “An exclusive interview from the rescuer herself, Hannah. She works at Janeris International and witnessed the accident from the sixth floor. Ma’am, can you tell me what you saw?”

I watched the woman talk about what she saw and decided she looked like she knew what to do. Grown-ups usually didn’t.

I wiped the last bit of chip dust off my hands onto my jeans and decided to find her.

I left the hospital and headed to Delaware Avenue, back to where I first met the woman.

CHAPTER ELEVEN

HANNAH

I PRESSED THE elevator button again. Everybody thinks the machine will move faster if you press three times instead of one. Today I agree with them.

Hurry up!

The doors opened slowly. I smashed the number six and paced corner to corner inside the rectangular box.

If I stop, I will feel it.

I had a plan. I focused on that certainty.

I hated lying to Ben and Lucy, but they'd learned when to step in and when to leave me be.

We hadn't chosen this bond — it was chosen for us, and I didn't know how I'd function without it now. Lucy understood me without a question; Ben made a point of standing between me and anything that might hurt me.

I wish I'd told him my plan so he'd show up unexpectedly, I thought as the elevator doors slid open onto the sixth floor of Janeris International.

You're only going to peek at Jerry's office. It's a great distraction.

He's not here to hurt you, I reminded myself. *Would he have hurt me, even with his finger on the trigger?*

I shook that image out of my head and glanced around the office floor. Debbi was in the conference room in a heated discussion on the phone.

Probably narrating the company's impending collapse to someone who didn't ask.

Harold was visible through the window on his office door, also on the phone. His head was in his hands and his shoulders slumped forward.

He looked less like a CEO and more like a man bracing for impact.

I decided it was now or never. I grabbed a stack of papers off a desk to my right and casually walked across the office like I was focused only on my work-related task.

Jerry's door loomed up in front of me as I set the papers down nearby.

Gulping, I twisted the door handle and pushed the door inward.

Mr. Leota glanced up at me with a hammer in his hand.

My mouth opened and I muffled a scream with my hand.

Jerry's office was torn apart. The computer screen was cracked, drawers dumped and papers scattered about. A computer tower was disassembled and the metal guts crushed across the desk.

"What, what are you doing?" I finally squeaked.

"Turn around and remind yourself you saw nothing. You don't want to make this worse for yourself," Mr. Leota said.

Something in his voice told me this wasn't about him being caught in Jerry's office.

It was the fact I was there, too.

Taking two steps towards me, he tightened his grip on the hammer.

I stumbled backwards and nodded, my eyes stretched wide.

"Yes, yes, of course. I saw nothing. I'm sorry I interrupted your *meeting*, Mr. Leota."

The door shut in front of me and I finally gasped out loud.

The office returned in pieces—fabric chairs, carpet squares, the humming lights. My feet moved before my brain caught up, carrying me back to my desk. I sat down out of habit and leaned my head on the back of the chair, wondering how long until Mr. Leota would come by to make sure I hadn't tattled.

How do I even prove I'm not going to say anything?

I felt a hand wrap around my ankle and the world slammed back into place.

A scream caught in my throat. I kicked hard, my chair skidding backwards as my pulse roared in my ears.

The little boy from the accident peeked out from under my desk, his hands wrapped tightly around his backpack.

"Oh my God, kid! You gave me a heart attack!"

Relief hit—then vanished.

Who else might be looking for him?

I had so many questions I wanted to ask.

Do I tell him I was at his house?

As I was formulating where to go from here, I heard Harold's voice. I shoved my chair forward, my knees hitting the boy's head. I shoved him deeper into the cavern of the desk.

Harold passed by and nodded at me, his eyes scanning my desk.

"Hi, Mr. Janeris," I said and pretended to be very focused on my dark computer screen, which thankfully faced away from the pedestrians.

Mr. Leota trailed closely behind Harold. I looked over at him. He raised his finger to his lips and made a shushing sound. Winking at me, he continued past me. My stomach felt like I was going to be sick.

I pretended to barely notice and continued to shuffle things around on my desk.

I looked around my cubicle wall to verify they'd disappeared somewhere and grabbed Lincoln's collar and dragged him to the women's restroom.

"Hey!' He protested.

"I'm sorry, but they can't see you," I said breathless.

"Why not?" Lincoln replied.

"Why are you here?" I asked, leaning over to see the boy at eye level.

"I found the guy," he replied as if I knew the entire story.

"What guy?"

"The one you pulled from the car. Don't you want to see him?"

"Who are you?" I asked.

"I'm Lincoln, the boy you saw on the sidewalk," he said.

Breathe, Hannah, I said to myself. *What are you really trying to say here?*

I took a deep breath then lowered myself onto my heels. I smiled at the boy who seemed very calm despite the fact he'd just snuck into a secure office.

"Do you want to see him or not?" Lincoln asked impatiently.

"Um, yeah, sure," I said, not really knowing what I was agreeing to.

The bathroom door opened and Lincoln hid behind me. Debbi stared at me long enough I stopped trying to read her face.

I heard Harold's voice at the same time as Debbi. She glanced behind her then quickly stepped into the bathroom and leaned her weight into the door to close it faster.

"Who is this young fellow?" Debbi asked. Her voice lifted into a practiced pitch, a tone meant to cover panic and pretend nothing is wrong.

"So sorry, Debbi. His mom is obsessed with not leaving him alone in the bathroom. It's silly, I know. Tommy, go do your thing so we can get you home," I said, trying to mirror Debbi's casual tone.

Lincoln looked at me embarrassed but thankfully obeyed. He walked into a stall and locked the door.

“That’s my sister’s kid. He had a half day at school for teacher conferences, and she asked if I could get him home,” I said, hoping to distract Debbi from the fact Lincoln hadn’t moved after locking the stall door.

Debbi continued to stare at me, so I babbled on.

“I’ll be gone for a few minutes, it’s been a day!” I tried to shrug but the tension hung so heavy I wasn’t sure my shoulders moved.

“You were late this morning, and left already once today,” Debbi said flatly.

“Hey, that ‘leaving’ wasn’t entirely my fault,” I snapped. “I happened to witness an accident. Had to give a statement. I came back as quickly as I could."

I was beginning to get annoyed with all this drama.

I'm sick of not understanding what's happening around me.

"Why did you stop me from defending myself back then?" I asked Debbi, leaning closer to her. I felt anger rolling around in my hands.

Debbi seemed to notice my demeanor changed and smiled sweetly at me.

"Nothing, you're right. It's fine. What a traumatic thing to experience! Don't have a thought of it again. Get your *nephew* safely home and report back immediately," she said pleasantly, rehearsed. "Hurry, please. You wouldn't want to be the reason this company shut down!" she said as if she were making a joke.

"Okay? Thanks, Debbi." I sensed there was more, but I knew better than to ask.

Debbi turned and left without using the toilet. Lincoln peeked out and asked if it was okay to come out.

"Yeah, thank you. Sorry, I didn't mean to embarrass you," I said patting Lincoln on the shoulder.

He smiled up at me then dropped to the floor and unzipped his backpack. He gathered a pile of fabric and handed it to me.

"You'll need to wear this," he said.

"What? Where'd you get this?" I said, holding up hospital scrubs. The logo stitched into the chest was recognizable.

"He's okay."

"Who?"

"The man."

"He was not okay when I saw him earlier," I said gravely, holding the scrubs against me.

"He was faking it."

"How do you know?"

"I saw him. He called me by name."

"You saw him?"

"Yes."

Enough denial, I told myself.

You've been looking for the boy and he found you. Now, follow him.

"Alright, fine. I'll change at the hospital."

I opened the door and stuffed the scrubs under my shirt. I looked around and grabbed Lincoln's hand.

With my purse carefully tucked in my arms, Lincoln and I headed toward the elevator.

"Hurry back, now," Debbi called from her desk. She smiled and waved.

Why does that sound like a warning?

For the third time that day, I hit the lobby button in the elevator.

CHAPTER TWELVE

LINCOLN

I TOOK A SEAT by the window, and Hannah stood in front of me, bracing herself with one hand on the pole, the other resting against the seat back near my shoulder. The bus jerked forward and she barely moved, like she'd been standing on buses her whole life. She kept her eyes ahead, not scared or confused—just focused.

This is what bravery looks like. Not asking questions. Not looking back. Keeping your chin up. Just deciding something and doing it.

The ride didn't take long, and she stayed steady the whole way. I figured she knew exactly where we were going and what would happen when we got there. Grown-ups usually did.

As the bus slowed, Hannah reached out for my hand and gestured for me to go first. I squeezed her hand as she hesitated. I think she dropped her purse or something, so I gave her a second before moving forward.

At the main entrance, she stopped.

"Do you know how to get to the guy's room?" she asked, staring ahead like she'd never seen automatic doors before.

I realized she was waiting for me the way kids wait for grown-ups.

I tugged her hand and headed for the sliding doors. "Yes, I do. But I recommend you plug your nose. It smells in here," I told her.

She followed, and I think she smiled a little.

"Where do you think I should change?" Hannah whispered behind me.

I'd forgotten about the nurse costume I'd stolen from the hospital during my last visit.

"I think there is a bathroom right near Eiden's room," I said.

"Eiden?"

"Yeah, that's his name."

"Oh."

We stopped in front of the elevator and Hannah adjusted the collar on my shirt like she'd done it a thousand times. When I looked up, she mumbled an apology and crossed her arms. I didn't mind.

We loaded the elevator with four other hospital people. I pressed the big number three.

The hospital workers discussed whether a patient should be isolated or left in ICU. They seemed bored by the conversation, but it sounded important to me.

Hannah stayed behind me with her hands on my shoulders, watching the numbers change. She guided me forward when the doors opened at three.

I led us to the bathroom and pointed.

"Are you okay out here for a moment?" she asked, scanning the hallway.

"Yeah, I'm good," I said, thinking about the free chips on the fifth floor.

She nodded and slipped inside. I dropped my backpack on the floor and pulled out the bag of food I'd brought from school. I hoped it was still good. I really needed to go home and feed Mom. I wasn't sure what time it was, but I bet it was way past school time and Mom would probably start to worry. I shoved the sack back inside and zipped up my backpack.

Hannah opened the door with a wild expression on her face, like she'd seen something bad. She looked like she needed me to hug her, but I didn't know her very well. I grabbed her hand and squeezed, like Mom does for me. She gave me a tiny smile, and I noticed her new outfit.

"You look like a real nurse, Hannah!" I said, shocked at her sudden transition.

Hannah's smile widened.

"It was a good idea, Lincoln. I admit I'm a little nervous. I've never faked a job before," she admitted.

I have a lot of good ideas, I thought, standing a little taller.

"Want to see an even bigger transformation?" Hannah said with a smirk.

I had no idea what she meant but I nodded.

She grabbed her curly hair with both hands and smoothed both sides of her head. She must have used a hair tie or ribbon, because when she lowered her hands, her hair stayed away from her face.

"I almost don't recognize you," I said in amazement. "It's perfect! We're definitely doing a matching costume for Halloween."

"Yeah, kid. That sounds good," she said.

Why did she look sad?

Maybe she would come to the school Halloween party next year. The kids at school would be so jealous of our matching costumes.

"Where is Eiden's room, Lincoln?"

"Oh yeah. It's 302, right over there," I replied, pointing two doors down the hall. Hannah started walking.

With her hair up, she looked older.

Hannah stopped abruptly outside Eiden's room, turned toward me, and leaned in to whisper something I couldn't hear. I was about to ask her what she said when I saw a real man nurse leave the room and look at Hannah.

"He needs an MRI of the brain with contrast, stat," the man said to Hannah's back.

I elbowed Hannah and she turned to face the nurse.

"What...doctor...is ordering it?" Hannah said, her words clipped.

The nurse in purple scrubs sighed heavily then said, "Dr. Jameison, duh."

He shoved a clipboard toward her. She took it and pulled it to her chest.

"Sure, got it. I will get those orders in...stat," Hannah replied, then strode into Eiden's room like she belonged. The purple nurse rolled his eyes again, then walked toward the nurse's station.

I didn't want to go back in the room with the man who knew my name.

Hannah did it, so I can too.

I lifted my chin a bit higher and dashed into the room. I stopped short at the foot of the bed. Hannah was flipping through the pages on the clipboard.

"How do you know all that doctor talk?" I asked, watching her lift her gaze to Eiden.

"I watch a lot of television shows, I guess. Never thought it'd help me in a real-life heist," she said wistfully. She was so focused on his face.

I turned away and noticed a dresser behind the door.

Maybe I can find something about Eiden in there.

I went to the first drawer and pulled.

A deep voice boomed so loud, I ducked against the corner of the dresser.

"Will he be awake soon?" The voice made me push myself against the dresser harder.

I hope he can't see me.

I pressed closer to the wall. His voice scared me.

Hannah's shoulders tensed, but she didn't turn towards the voice. I couldn't see the man from where I was hiding.

Hannah began to talk like she was in a school play—lighthearted, slightly annoyed, and consistent. She didn't turn to look at the man in the doorway.

"No, sir. His brain is swelling. He's in a medically induced coma for an unknown amount of time. No visitors, please. We're about to do a stat brain MRI to get us more information. Please leave your contact information with the nurse's station for further updates."

Hannah's voice didn't sound like hers anymore. It was lower, confident.

Adults listen to that sort of voice, I thought, watching her hold her posture just like on the bus.

The man said an adult word under his breath, and I heard his footsteps moving away. His steps sounded angry and short.

"Is his brain really swelling? Is he going to die?" I said from my corner.

Hannah turned to me, and I felt silly for being afraid. She waved me over and I went. She wrapped her arms around my shoulders.

"No, sweetheart. That was a bad man. I lied."

That's what bravery sounds like.

A hand reached out for Hannah's arm and I backed away. The hand was draped with plastic and wires. It grabbed Hannah's wrist and pulled her toward him.

Eiden.

The man in the car accident.

The man that saved me.

The beeps from the machines around Eiden started to climb—fast, sharp—like my very own heartbeat jumping inside my chest.

I didn't notice if Hannah was surprised like me, but she stepped closer to the man in the bed. They were staring at each other. Hannah's shoulders relaxed, like she was watching her favorite cartoon.

"I'm sorry, sir. Thank you, for...getting hurt for me," I babbled. I felt silly. I wanted to have a better apology, but I forgot what I'd planned.

Both the adults glanced at me. Hannah smiled, then looked back at the man.

I slipped behind Hannah and grabbed the edge of her shirt. She grabbed my hand with her other hand.

"You found him," Eiden said.

"He found me," Hannah whispered.

Is she crying? Why is she quiet all of a sudden?

"Hide him. This wasn't an accident. They want him," Eiden said louder.

Hide him? Hide me?

"Who wants him? Who are you?" Hannah asked.

"I'm Eiden," the man replied.

I had been wondering about that.

“Like the Garden of Eden?” I asked. “Your name is spelled wrong.”

Eiden smirked and nodded in agreement. I stepped to the side so Eiden could see me better.

“How do you know me?” I asked.

Eiden’s smile went into a frown and he didn’t answer.

I heard a heavy footstep in the hallway and thought about diving under Eiden’s bed.

“Hannah, I think that bad guy is coming back,” I said, tugging on her shirt again. I didn’t know how I knew it was the same bad guy, but I *felt* him.

"Leota," Hannah said as she seemed to see something outside of me for a moment.

Leota?

"You know Leota?" Eiden said, as he forced himself upright.

"Sort of," Hannah said. "He's the security guard in my office."

Eiden's eyes flickered to me, then back to Hannah.

"You shouldn't have brought him here," Eiden said, his voice hard. "You need to go, now."

"Hey, don't be mean to Hannah," I said stepping forward.

"Why? What am I even doing with him?" Hannah said.

She pulled me against her and put her hands on my shoulders.

"Go. Protect Lincoln. Keep him safe. Stay away from me. I'll be there as soon as I can."

"So, you're okay?"

"I'm fine. Stop wasting time with stupid questions!"

"But you were nearly dead when I pulled you out of the car!"

Hannah seemed like she was going to cry so I turned around and hugged her waist.

She patted my back and kissed my head.

"It's okay, Lincoln. He's right at least in some ways. We need to leave, now."

I heard Eiden take a deep breath behind me, and I glanced back at him.

"I will explain later. Just keep him safe. Kid, listen to her, please?"

I nodded as the angry footsteps grew closer.

"Hannah, he's almost here!"

I was about to tell Hannah to crawl under the man's bed when she let go of me.

No, no, come back!

I squeezed my eyes shut and covered them. I heard someone slap the wall and sirens sounded around us. I opened my eyes to see Hannah running back at me. She grabbed my elbow and pulled me to the doorway.

A speaker crackled overhead: "Code Blue: Room 302. Code Blue: Room 302. All available personnel please respond."

We sprinted down the hallway. Two doorways past where we started, Hannah put her hands on my stomach and shoved me sideways.

I stumbled into a dark room, and she fell in beside me.

CHAPTER THIRTEEN

LINCOLN

"Sorry, bud. Shh!"

Hannah stood up and reached out for my hand. She guided me to the dark side of the doorway and put her finger to her lips. I nodded that I understood.

I had heard the footsteps. I knew the bad man passed us again, along with several other costumed workers.

A nurse yelled, "Sir, please leave!"

I wanted to look around the corner, but Hannah stopped me and shook her head left and right.

I heard the mean man's steps coming back toward us and pressed my face into Hannah.

She held me tightly for a few moments, then released me.

"He's gone, Lincoln. I need to change," she said. "Are you okay hiding in that corner for a moment? I promise I'll be fast."

I peered into the dark room and saw a spot by the dresser like the one where I'd hidden in Eiden's room. I walked over and sat down on the cold ground, crisscross applesauce.

Hannah glanced at me again, like she had to be certain I was okay, then disappeared into the bathroom.

True to her promise, Hannah returned quickly. She was wearing a purple jacket, and her hair was loose again. She walked over to me and patted my shoulder.

"I can't take you back to work with me, Lincoln. And don't ask me why, because I don't even know yet," Hannah said then paused. She looked at my backpack and then at my eyes again. "How old are you?"

"Eight," I replied, putting on my backpack and standing as tall as I could.

"I have to go back, and I have to get there before Leota returns," she said. She knelt in front of me with a frown. "You can't go to your house, either."

I stepped back.

"Why not? Mom needs her food!"

Hannah reached out again and patted my shoulder. I didn't resist. I wasn't mad at her.

"Because, I think you're in danger, but I don't know why. I would like to help, if you're okay with that."

"I'm in danger? Because of what Eiden said?"

"Yeah, buddy. I know we don't know him, but I think I trust him. What do you think?"

She turned her head sideways and waited for my reply. Her eyes darted back and forth over my face.

What do I think?

I pictured Eiden on the stretcher grabbing Hannah's hand, then doing it again in the hospital room. He seemed very serious. Very certain. And Hannah trusted him.

"I guess that works for me. But I need to feed Mom before bedtime, okay?" I pointed at my backpack.

"I'm not promising anything, Lincoln. But if it's in my power, I will make sure your mom is okay."

We stepped towards the doorway together. Her hand tightened around mine as we moved from the darkness into the artificial brightness of the hallway.

CHAPTER FOURTEEN

HANNAH

I PROMISED A kid I'd protect him.

I knew nothing about how to care for a kid—domestically or otherwise.

Where do I hide him? How do I hide him? I should have read more books this year.

I pulled Lincoln into the elevator, praying Mr. Leota was gone, when my phone vibrated.

Debbi.

WHERE ARE YOU?? GET HERE ASAP. 911.

My stomach dropped. Debbi never used language like that.

What was happening at the office? Did Mr. Leota rip apart my desk?

I typed back that I was on my way.

"I really have to get back to work as fast as possible. Didn't you say the bus was faster than a car?"

"Yeah, because of the special bus alleys that cars aren't supposed to drive down," Lincoln said, following me like we were heading to the zoo.

Why does he trust me? What if I do something wrong and he gets hurt?

Debbi's 911 text pressed against my skull, demanding I think faster.

"You can't go to my office, and you can't go to your house..." I said out loud trying to discover a mathematical formula that hadn't yet been invented. "Can you go back to school?"

I pictured his mom fussing at me that it's school hours and realized I had no idea what time school hours were.

"No, I think it got out a few minutes ago," Lincoln said with a shrug.

"Do you know the deli by my office?"

"Yes," Lincoln said hesitantly. His shoulder sagged forward as we stopped by the bus.

"Go there and tell them you need to pick up an order for me. Pick something that will take a little time. I'll go into the office. I'll play sick or something and then come get you there. How does that sound?"

I felt a little helpless. I glanced back at the hospital's third floor windows.

Are you really going to come find us and help? Because I have no idea what I'm doing.

“I can’t do that, Hannah,” Lincoln said, looking at his shoes.

“What’s up, buddy?” I asked. He looked so small, so young. I wanted to hug him again and tell him everything would be okay. But I hated lying.

“Deli devil hates me. She shoos me away whenever I go around there,” Lincoln said, looking defeated.

I couldn’t help but laugh out loud. Lincoln looked up at me surprised.

“Sorry,” I said with a smile that came from deep inside me. “I didn’t have the best experience with her earlier, either. But you know what?”

Lincoln’s eyes lit with curiosity as he adjusted the straps on his shoulders.

"Her husband is the reason I found you."

A small smile spread across Lincoln's face as the bus arrived.

"He feeds me breakfast sometimes," Lincoln said. "Where do you live?"

Of course, why didn't I think of that?

"I live just a few blocks from my office, but the bus line isn't running right now. I can unlock the door from my phone. Want to hang out with my cat for a while?"

"You have a cat?" Lincoln said brightening. He asked me more questions about my cat and if she was nice and would he be allowed to hold her. I answered his questions best I could, but

I'd never seen my cat with a kid, so I told him I wasn't sure.

"Do you know how to follow turn-by-turn directions?" I said as we stepped off the bus. I felt better that we had a plan. I didn't like sending this kid back out alone, but I had no choice. And Debbi's text weighed on me.

"Of course. I'm eight, you know," Lincoln said, facing me with his hands on his hips.

"Yes, you are. Very mature," I said with a smile. "You only have to remember two turns. And please wait for the crosswalk lights, okay?"

"I know. Hey, I have a notebook in my backpack. Hang on." Lincoln bent down and dug in his backpack. He stood back up with a pen and paper pad at ready.

This kid is just too much.

It scared me how fast he'd taken root in my heart.

"Go north on this street, Delaware Avenue," I began, pointing up the street, "until you get to West Tupper. Cross over Tupper and turn right. My apartment building is the first building on your left."

He scribbled furiously to keep up. When he slowed, I continued.

"Just walk in that front door as confidently as you did at the hospital and you'll be fine. In the elevator, go to the second floor. I'm in 202. The front door will be unlocked. Please lock the door once you get in? That's how I will know you're safe. I will be home by 5:30 at the latest, and then I'll make you dinner."

Lincoln dropped his pen and paper in his backpack, then stood back up. He looked at me for a split second, then dropped his head against my stomach. He wrapped his arms around me and took a deep breath. I hugged him back. He turned and walked away.

I hope this is the right choice.

I watched him leave. My breath stuttered once and fear flickered–quick and unreasonable–then settled.

Debbi's 911 surfaced, reminding me there was no room for panic right now.

Mr. Leota would return any moment, and I could not be outside when he arrived.

I barely noticed my sweating palms as I ascended to floor six. The doors slid open and Debbi jumped at me, grabbing my arm and didn't let go until she'd shoved me into a chair in the conference room.

"Take these, quick!" Debbi said, thrusting a notepad and pen toward me. She slammed the door shut and sat down across from me with her own notepad.

I glanced down as I held the notepad and saw several lines of scrawled notes.

"But, what..." I wanted to ask but stopped as the door flung open and Mr.

Leota and Harold stomped in. Mr. Leota walked over to me and glared down. I didn't glance up, but I felt his stare boiling through my scalp.

"Excuse us, gentlemen, we have a very strict deadline," Debbi said, annoyance edging in her voice.

"Catch me up on where we're at, please," Harold said, glancing over at Mr. Leota, at me, then Debbi. He rubbed his hands together like he couldn't warm up.

"Once we are done here, Hannah will send you the summary as always," Debbi said making it clear the men weren't supposed to be there.

"We still don't have today's mail," Mr. Leota said. His voice was soft, but my body responded like his words were a threat. I forced myself to continue to stare at my notes.

"You know how Fridays are, Mr. Janeris," Debbi said with a smile, ignoring Mr. Leota. "We'll be caught up before end of day."

"Beijing is behind on the shipment for the Vanisck's file, but they have been notified of our impatience. The client has been made aware," I began, scanning the notes furiously for something that Harold wouldn't have seen in my last report.

"Gentlemen?" Debbi said, her glasses barely secured to the tip of her nose.

Mr. Leota finally gave up boiling my scalp and I continued talking about the case with Debbi.

The men left and shut the door.

Debbi whispered, "Why'd you have to get involved? What are you thinking?"

"Involved in what? I have no idea what's going on," I said, throwing my hands up in the air.

"Lincoln!"

"You know him?" I leaned closer to her.

"That's Harold's nephew!"

"What! That druggie is Harold's sister?" I felt instantly bad about branding the woman. "I mean, that woman...why didn't you say you knew him when you saw him?"

"You met Renee? You've got yourself in some shit, Hannah. Dammit! Where is Lincoln now?"

Renee. That's a beautiful name.

"I don't know," I lied. "I'm not his mother! What's happening?"

"Where'd you take him?"

"Lincoln needed a ride," I said, deciding not to trust anybody anymore, but I hated lying.

"To where? You don't have a car."

I struggled to understand Debbi's sudden intensity. Her tone was usually too happy or excited, like she had the most exciting news to share and was dying for you to ask about it.

“I took the bus with him,” I replied honestly, trying to read this new side of the woman I’d worked with for years.

“Where’d you go?” Debbi pressed.

“Why does it matter? What’s the big deal? And what’s up with Mr. Leota today? He’s everywhere!”

I gave away too much.

Debbi leaned back in her chair and restored her usual fake demeanor.

“It’s nothing, Hannah. Stay away from Lincoln and Renee. They’re bad news. Now get those notes to Harold and make sure that damn mail gets distributed!”

CHAPTER FIFTEEN

LINCOLN

I FOUND HANNAH'S apartment building exactly as she told me. The doorman looked up when I came through the front door, but I just did what Hannah told me to do. This was no different than the hospital. I pretended I was seventeen and had been here many times. I think the doorman believed me.

The elevator was more challenging because the numbers were laid out differently than the hospitals, but I figured it out.

I missed Hannah's front door a couple of times and walked up and down the hallway, but eventually found it and walked in. Once inside, I locked the door, just like I promised I would.

I heard a meow. A grey-and-black cat with a white heart on its head peeked around the corner. I put my backpack down and called for it to come to me. I hadn't touched a cat in a very long time. I hoped it would like me. The cat got closer and I knelt, reaching out with both hands. It got close enough that I scooped it up in my arms. I leaned my head against its furry ears. The cat leaned into my nose, and I almost sneezed.

"You must be Juliet," I said out loud, remembering what Hannah had told me. The cat responded by making a noise I'd heard was called purring.

Still holding the vibrating cat, I wandered farther down the entryway. There were pretty things hanging from the walls and bright green plants spilling over their pots.

To my left I saw a couch and television. On the small table by the couch were shiny picture frames. I walked closer, scratching the cat's ears.

One photograph was a younger Hannah, wearing a sports jersey and a smirk that made her look very strong. Another showed her clutching a ball and standing between two smiling adults who looked like parents. More recent photos showed Hannah with a guy and girl about her age. The girl was blonde and the boy looked serious. Hannah smiled without her teeth in all the photos but looked happy.

The cat started wiggling in my arms, so I figured she needed to eat or use her toilet. I set her carefully on the ground. I followed her to the other side of the apartment, which led to the kitchen. I opened the fridge and felt overwhelmed with all the options. I reached for the raspberry jelly. I located peanut butter and bread and made myself a sandwich.

Just a snack. Hannah said she'd make dinner. She had just the right things for a snack.

I sat at the table and watched the cat wander around while I ate. When I was done, I wiped up my crumbs and washed the knife. I followed the cat around for a few minutes before sitting down on the couch. I thought maybe I'd turn on the television, but the blanket I'd found on the back of the couch was heavy and warm. Juliet jumped up on the couch and snuggled against my chest. I sank lower.

I drifted off to sleep wondering what sort of dinner Hannah would make.

CHAPTER SIXTEEN

HANNAH

FIVE NEVER FELT so late.

I glanced up from my desk and saw the rain snaking across the windows. The sun was already down, and I knew the walk home was going to be miserable.

I don't care how long I live here, I'll never get used to cold rain. Can't it just snow? Snow is soft and gentle. Rain is so intrusive.

I knew I needed to grow up and get a car, but when the bus route was running it was only one stop between work and my apartment. Unfortunately, both bus routes were temporarily closed due to construction. The project was only supposed to have been six months, but it'd felt like six years.

Especially during the winter.

The forecast predicted lake effect snow the next two days. Buffalo and the towns to the south could easily be buried under feet of snow with a forecast like that. I guess I should have been happy it was raining, and not yet frozen.

I started thinking about what I'd do when I got home. I hoped Lincoln was comfortable. I'd seen the notification that my deadbolt had closed only a few minutes after he'd left me, so I knew he was in the apartment.

I was about to enter the elevator when Harold walked in front of me and held his hands against the doors, like he'd been planning this moment.

I mumbled a thank you and stepped into the elevator, clutching my purse. My jaw tightened as Harold stepped in followed closely by Mr. Leota.

"It looks gross outside," Harold said, staring up at the descending numbers.

"Yeah, it does," I said, pretending that I didn't feel awkward and anxious.

"Let me drive you home?" Harold asked.

"Ah, no thanks, Mr. Janeris. I already called my Uber," I lied.

That makes two lies today.

Harold nodded like he'd already expected that answer. Mr. Leota glanced at Harold then at me.

"Good work today, Hannah. Sorry about obsessing over the mail. I was expecting something important today that just didn't make it. Guess I'll have to wait until Monday," he said with a small tilt of his head. He seemed to be watching me for a reaction.

"What should I be on the lookout for? I can make sure to bring it immediately on Monday," I said, turning to face him, like I was genuinely happy to help.

I don't know why I offered that. Mail was usually first, but today my routine had been shredded.

"Uh, no, it's okay," Harold said. "Normal processing is understandable with the workload you all handle." He chuckled and Mr. Leota glared at the back of his head.

Thankfully the elevator doors screeched open, and he gestured to allow me to exit first.

"Goodnight, Mr. Janeris. Have a good weekend," I said. I hesitated inside the front door, making a show of tying my scarf and putting on gloves.

"Hannah," he replied, tipping his head.

I nodded back.

Mr. Leota grunted as he walked by and I imagined he said something meant only for me.

I raised my hand in a silly wave and flashed an awkward smile.

Why does it feel like Monday will be a very different workday?

I delayed for several minutes, hoping that Harold and Mr. Leota were gone, then I started my miserable journey home. Five blocks aren't bad until sideways ice-rain soaks every pore of my body and the umbrella does little against the wind.

A few minutes into my walk, my phone vibrated. I ripped off a glove to fish my phone out of my pocket. There was a text from Lucy waiting.

ANYMORE TEA TO SPILL ABOUT MONSTERS IN POCKETS OR WHATEVER IT WAS?

My phone was getting soaked and my fingers were numb, so I responded quickly.

**JUST GETTING OUT OF WORK...
WILL TEXT SOON**

I was about to put the phone back in my pocket when I felt it vibrate again.

BEN WANTS TO KNOW IF WE'RE STILL ON FOR TOMORROW?

I put the phone back in my pocket, telling myself I'd respond to Lucy when I got home. I didn't want to think about tomorrow yet.

Another block and I began to wonder why I hadn't ordered that Uber I'd lied about — and whether it was too late to turn back.

I tried to focus on Lincoln and Renee, and how to protect Lincoln.

One step at a time, Hannah.

I'd make dinner and get to know him more. Give him the attention he'd likely been missing. Maybe ask him if he had homework we should work on.

Then after sleeping tonight, I'd make a plan. I was so tired and frozen.

I turned the corner to my apartment complex and pulled on the front door. The night doorman had always watched for me and unlatched the lock before I'd tug on the door. Tonight, the door resisted and I peered into the vestibule. The doorman wasn't at his desk.

I walked to the side of the front door and entered a code then rushed back to the door as it buzzed. Walking through the silent atrium was eerie. Juan, the night watchman, had always been on duty by now, but his desk sat empty. I walked quickly through the foyer, feeling like I didn't belong. I punched the door close button on the elevator as soon as I boarded.

I wonder what Lincoln is doing.

The elevator delivered me to the second floor.

I typed in the code for my door and pushed it inwards. The entryway was darker than I left it this morning.

I stepped over the threshold and quietly shut the door behind me.

The apartment was too silent.

I tightened my grip on the umbrella.

I took one step inside, then froze.

Jerry stood in the hallway.

A kitchen knife rested in his right hand, blade down.

CHAPTER SEVENTEEN

HANNAH

"JERRY?!" I SAID, raising my umbrella like a jousting stick.

"Hannah, did you get my message?" Jerry said. He looked down at the floor and lowered the knife to his side.

I raised the umbrella again and shoved it toward him.

"Message?" I said. I had no idea who to trust. "Where is Lincoln? Lincoln!"

Lincoln walked into the hallway from the kitchen, my cat in one arm and a bite of popcorn in the other.

"Yeah?" he replied, tossing the popcorn into his mouth and adjusting his hold on my ever-patient cat.

Lincoln looked relaxed. Safe.

"Lock the door and come sit down. You're drenched. Dinner is ready," Jerry said.

"Dinner? Jerry! You tried to kill us!" I said thoroughly confused. Lincoln took a step toward me and tilted his head.

"Jerry wouldn't kill anybody, silly," Lincoln said matter of fact, then turned and disappeared into the kitchen.

The way Lincoln said it—so certain, I decided it was time to be angry. I was tired of being in the dark, sick of everybody knowing what was happening except me.

"What the hell, Jerry! What are you doing here?"

"I didn't want to kill anybody, Hannah. That's not what happened," Jerry said, still staring at the floor. "I was just making dinner. I think I need to check the stove, if it's okay for me to move now." He eyed my umbrella.

He has a knife and I'm holding an umbrella, but I'm the threat?

"Okay?" I said, following him hesitantly to the kitchen.

Lincoln had set Juliet on the floor and poured food into her dish. The cat was happily munching away and Lincoln sat down at the table.

"Hannah, it's not raining inside. Put down the umbrella and sit," Lincoln said, like he was my father.

I felt like I was becoming numb to surprises. The knife was safely in the sink, so I leaned the umbrella against the wall and sat down as instructed.

"I think you'll like dinner, Hannah. I helped!" Lincoln said proudly.

Jerry glanced over at him from the stove and smiled, then served three plates with stuffed chicken and a side of broccoli smothered in mozzarella.

The food smelled amazing and I realized I'd only eaten a pastry from Huron Street Deli all day.

"This is good," I said. Lincoln nodded.

This feels absurd.

After a few minutes of eating and awkward silence, I decided I needed more answers.

"So, I did get your message, Jerry," I began. "I assumed the note meant this coming Sunday...at the prerelease in Orchard Park; I remember you talking about that collector's card game a lot.

But today is Friday. How did you know where I lived?"

Jerry beamed at me like he was so proud I'd solved his clue.

"I wasn't sure how much you'd listened to me talk about those monsters, but I am happy I was right about how much you cared. You were the only coworker that saw me, really."

"Jerry, why are you here?" I asked. I didn't have time to pat him on the head.

"The accident. It moved up my timeline."

"Timeline for what?"

Jerry tilted his head towards Lincoln.

"How do you know him?"

"Well, I don't know him directly."

"Hey, Lincoln, do you want to go finish your dinner in front of the TV? I can turn on something cool!" I suggested. I knew nothing about raising a kid, but I felt the misunderstood tension in the air and worried about him.

"Ma'am, I'd like to stay if that's okay. I'm curious, too," Lincoln said apologetically.

I couldn't help myself. I reached across the corner of the table and waited for him to place his palm in mine. When he did, I squeezed and nodded. He smiled back at me and sat up straighter. I respected this kid. He'd been forced to grow up way earlier than some kids, but I understood him completely.

I recognized the posture, the listening-too-closely—it was the same way I'd learned to sit at tables where unfamiliar adults decided my life for me.

"I...I want to apologize," Jerry said, breaking the silence. "How I acted in the moment...the choice I was given...wasn't right. But I was set up. I think he knew I'd react that way. It was part of the plan. He knew I suspected. Now, at the very least, Leota will assume you know and he'll find a way to get rid of you." Jerry breathed deeply.

"Am I the only one that doesn't know what the hell I supposedly know?" I said, leaning back in my seat. "First the accident, then Eiden, then Debbi and Mr. Leota..."

"Leota... he'll assume you know and he'll find a way to get rid of you," Jerry repeated. "What about Debbi?"

"Interesting you ask," I said, glancing at Lincoln. He appeared to be handling this conversation well. "She saw Lincoln in the office and pretended she didn't know him until later when she told me I'd gotten myself into some...stuff."

"Lincoln was in the office? Did Leota see him?" Jerry said, his fork and knife at the ready above his chicken.

"I don't think so," I said honestly.

"So, then you know who Lincoln is, don't you," Jerry said, looking me in the eye.

I again glanced at Lincoln. I didn't know what he knew. He set his fork down quietly and folded his hands in his lap.

I put my hand out and waved him over. He came over and sat in my lap.

"You sure you're okay, buddy?"

Lincoln nodded but leaned into me.

"Yes, he's Harold's nephew. So?" I said quietly.

Lincoln looked up at me with a question behind his eyes but stayed quiet. I pulled him tighter against me, like I was telling him I'd explain once I understood myself.

Jerry seemed to notice how difficult this conversation might be for a kid and walked around to my side of the table. He knelt in front of Lincoln and pulled the kid's chin up to his own.

"Hey kid, your momma is amazing. She really is. You have an uncle who lives close. He's actually Hannah's boss, believe it or not. He used to be my boss, too. He is not amazing. He's a very bad guy. Your momma made a deal with him several years ago to leave you alone...to stay away."

Lincoln was quiet for a moment. Not sure I'd have handled this situation the way Jerry did, but who knew what the right thing was anymore.

"Is he the bad guy at the hospital asking about Eiden?" Lincoln asked, looking at me.

"You guys say Eiden?" Jerry asked, like we were talking about a Hollywood celebrity.

"No, hon, the bad guy is my boss's bodyguard," I told Lincoln.

I can only imagine how Lincoln feels right now. I'm basically twenty-one and I'm freaking out.

"Why does your boss have a bodyguard?"

Jerry snorted.

"Something...bad...happened in our office, and my boss, Mr. Janeris, hired a security team to protect all of us," I said with a sad smile towards Jerry.

"What happened?" Lincoln said.

I was saved from a response by a quiet knock on the door, quickly followed by an aggressive tapping.

"Let me in!" I heard a man's voice yell.

I jumped up and told Lincoln to hide in the pantry.

Jerry nodded. He grabbed Lincoln and closed them both in the pantry.

"Hurry!" The voice said from the atrium.

I felt like I'd heard the voice before.

"Who is it?" I called out, grabbing my umbrella and approaching the door.

"Eiden! Who else! Open. The. Door!"

Eiden! He came to help with Lincoln!

I rushed to open the door. Eiden shoved me back and shut the door, locking the single deadbolt.

He stared at it for a moment like he'd never seen a digital lock.

"How does everybody know where I live?" I said, dropping my umbrella.

"The internet," Eiden said. He faced me. "Good timing with your nurse act, by the way. I was about to be discharged, and you screwed it up."

"What?"

"Where is the boy?"

"Hiding. I didn't screw it up, I made Leota leave," I insisted, putting my hands on my hips.

"No, you gave Leota a trail," Eiden said. "Get the boy. We have to leave now."

"You told me to protect him! I did!"

Eiden stepped closer.

"You didn't protect him," Eiden said, barely above a whisper. "You marked him."

I stepped back, my heel catching on the edge of the rug. I nodded, realizing that I had no choice anymore. Even though I understood nothing, I knew Lincoln was in danger—and that we'd all brought him here.

We were all responsible.

CHAPTER EIGHTEEN

LINCOLN

I THINK JERRY is more scared than I am.

His right foot was bouncing like mine did that one time I had to go up front of the class and write a subtraction problem on the chalkboard. But I agree it feels weird to be sitting in a pantry. I wish I'd grabbed the cat. But I've heard cats have a natural ability to hide when bad things happen.

I glanced up at Jerry's face. He had his knees up to his chest and his arms locked around his legs. His curly hair bounced above his forehead in time with the movement of his foot.

I heard the front door slam and wondered who had knocked, but I assumed if Hannah opened the door, it must be someone safe. I heard a man's voice and Hannah's voice raise. I didn't like how Hannah sounded. Her voice was tight, like she was mad, or annoyed. I wished I could hold her hand like she did for me earlier.

"This is your only lock? Shit. Get him, we have to leave!" I heard the man say, then footsteps approached.

Who is him? Hannah's cat is a girl.

"What? Why?" Hannah said, closer now.

"Hurry! No time! Where's your back door?"

The guy from the car and the hospital! He's here!

"I have a fire escape into a courtyard," Hannah said.

"Good, let's go!"

"My cat!"

"Nobody cares about a stupid cat... get the boy and get out!"

I'm the "him". Why do we have to leave? Wait, I can't leave without Mom's food!

I smacked Jerry on the arm and jumped up. I shoved open the pantry door as Hannah reached for the door handle.

"I have to get something first!"

I ran past Hannah, through the kitchen, to the living room.

"Lincoln, wait!" Jerry called after me.

I grabbed Mom's school lunch from the coffee table then turned around and ran into Jerry who had followed me.

"Sorry, Jerry."

Jerry grabbed my hand and pulled me back into the kitchen where Hannah stood with a cat carrier in her arms and a stubborn tilt to her lips.

Eiden asked Hannah something I couldn't hear and she pointed to a window on the side of the kitchen, near a closet.

"Let's go, everybody! Out the window!"

This man is like my principal, telling everybody what to do. I bet Hannah doesn't like that very much, I guessed. But then I heard it and I knew why Eiden was being bossy.

I fell to the floor without meaning to.

"Lincoln!" Hannah yelled and dove over me. My ears were piercing like the school period bell, but it didn't stop.

Bullets sound different in movies.

"Hannah! Get him!" Jerry said.

"Lincoln, are you okay?" Hannah said pushing my hair from my forehead.

I am, but I can't seem to talk. Hannah reached under my arms and lifted me partially off the floor and we both crawled over to where Eiden and Jerry were waiting by an open window.

It was hard to hear what the adults were saying, because glass was breaking and bullets were flying from somewhere in the entryway.

"What the hell!" Hannah said as she looked over her shoulder and pushed me towards Eiden. Eiden picked me up and set me on the other side of the window.

Jerry grabbed my hand, and I dropped the paper bag.

"Wait!" I said, finally able to speak. "I need the bag!"

"No time, Lincoln!" Jerry yelled as he tugged on my hands and another round of bullets sprayed into the kitchen.

"I need to feed my mom!" I was crying again.

Twice in one day!

Hannah picked me up. She turned me around and I buried my face in her neck.

"We will feed her, my love," Hannah whispered in my ear as she stepped carefully down the fire escape holding me tight. "Ssh, I've got you."

"Ah! Go, go, go!" I peeked over Hannah's shoulder and saw Eiden following closely to Hannah, a cat carrier in his hands extended arm's length from his chest.

"Where's your car?" Eiden yelled as they descended the final turn on the metal stairs.

"I don't have one," Hannah yelled back. She set me down and pointed to a ladder. Jerry stood at the bottom and reached his hands up to catch me.

I told my legs to work and began to climb down.

"But I know of a car we can use!"

All four of us were at the bottom of the ladder when the window over the sink exploded. Hannah put her hands over my head and Eiden stood over her.

"Over here!" Hannah said, grabbing my hand and running towards the corner of the building.

Turning the corner of the brick building, she quickly keyed in a PIN code at a gate. The gate beeped and she swung inwards. We all ran in and Jerry shut the gate. A blue car that looked older than the downtown church sat in front of us. The words on the side of the car read Oldsmobile Cutlass Sierra.

"This is my neighbor's car," Hannah said, searching the top of the front tire. "He once told me I could use it in an emergency. He was a kook, but here we are."

Eiden stepped in front of Hannah and grabbed the keys from her hand.

I opened the back door and slid in before Hannah.

Eiden shoved the cat carrier to me and I managed to grab it before it toppled to the street. Juliet mewed in disagreement. Hannah took the cat carrier from my lap as Eiden started the car, then set Juliet down by my feet.

"Buckle, Lincoln, please," Hannah said. Juliet meowed again.

I barely heard my seatbelt click before the car lurched forward and took its first turn too fast.

Hannah reached for my hand. I squeezed her fingers. In front of me, Jerry grabbed a handle above his head and buckled his seatbelt with a shaky hand.

“Down!” Eiden said as the back window shattered and landed all around me. I heard more gunshots and Hannah laid on top of me again. Juliet was making a lot of noise, so I put my hand on the carrier and whispered that I’d take care of her.

We drove in a straight line for a few minutes then Eiden said an adult word and we were suddenly driving the opposite direction.

Bullets tore through the side window. Spiderweb cracks raced across the glass.

"It's almost over, buddy, you're doing awesome," Hannah whispered to me. She didn't sound very confident, but I knew that even adults got scared sometimes.

"Does anybody have a phone?" Eiden yelled as he took a hard left turn, toppling Hannah even further onto me. She was kind of squishing me, but it felt safe for now.

"My phone is in the apartment. It was the cat or my phone," Hannah said flatly.

"I left mine in the apartment, too," Jerry added.

Eiden suddenly decelerated to a slow speed and Hannah and I slipped forward, only kept from landing on the floor by our seatbelts.

"Stay down back there," Jerry said as the bullets stopped hitting the car.

"Shit," Eiden said again.

"My mom has a phone we can use, Eiden," I said, careful not to say his name wrong. "And I really need to feed her."

"Shit," Eiden said again.

Juliet mewed from her carrier. I unzipped a corner to pet her head. I felt her begin to purr as she lay down.

"Fine, Lincoln, we'll go by your house. I need to check on her anyways."

I can't remember the last time an adult agreed with me without arguing or asking more questions. Even my teachers didn't believe me this morning when I told them there'd been an accident and that was why I was late—and it was true!

"Seriously?" Hannah said popping her head up.

I sat up and saw a car accident on the side of the road and police cruisers with their roof lights flashing blue and red.

"Hannah, isn't that your apartment building?" I said, recognizing where we were. We must have driven in a big circle.

"Yeah, buddy, that was my home," Hannah said glancing up at the building.

I reached over and grabbed her hand. I expected her to cry but she looked over and made a sad smile then squeezed my hand back.

"I'm sorry about your home, Hannah," I said. I felt like maybe I might cry, too.

"Eiden, do you know my mom?" I asked.

"Um... yeah. We're old friends," Eiden replied.

CHAPTER NINETEEN

LINCOLN

"EIDEN?" I ASKED. My whole body felt like what I imagined an earthquake felt like—everything was shaking.

This is cool: I got shot at, and I think we were in a car chase, but we won. And nobody got hurt. That means that, most likely, we will all be okay.

I don't know what I'll feed mom, but Hannah said she'd take care of her.

"What is it, Lincoln?" Eiden said after a moment.

"Did we lose the bad guys?" I asked.

"For now, yes," Eiden said.

"What are we going to feed Mom?"

Eiden didn't reply at first and I wondered if he'd heard me. Hannah looked over at me and put her hand over my arm like she was about to console me when Eiden lifted a familiar brown paper bag into the air.

Hannah dropped her hand to her lap and stared at Eiden.

"Thank you, sir," I said, relieved.

Eiden set the paper bag down on the front seat by Jerry and put both hands on the steering wheel. His eyebrows gathered on his forehead and he stared ahead like he needed glasses to see.

It wasn't long before we arrived at my house. I asked Hannah if I should bring Juliet in but she shook her head no.

"I don't think we will stay here, Lincoln," Hannah said.

"Come with me, Lincoln," Eiden said. "But we need to be quick."

I got out of the car and Eiden handed me the bag. The bottom corner was ripped so I held it tight against my chest and let Eiden into the house. I wanted to check on Mom first, but Eiden pointed to the bag and then the kitchen. I nodded and turned left to put the food away. I didn't know what the limit was for food being out of the fridge, but adults always said it mattered.

I heard a thud coming from Mom's room and threw the food in the fridge.

Eiden started shouting at Renee, something about getting it together and somebody needing to step up.

"Stop, Eiden! Stop yelling at her! She's sick!" I ran into Mom's room and leaned over her head, my back to Eiden.

"She's sick all right, Lincoln," Eiden said sternly. "She can't take care of herself let alone take care of you."

"We're just fine!" I buried my head into Mom's neck. I felt her shift then her hand wrapped around mine.

Eiden breathed deeply and stepped back.

"You need to stay with someone else until this is over, Lincoln," he finally said.

Mom's hand squeezed mine. I heard her try to say something, so I looked up at her face. Her eyes were open and her lips were moving, but instead of sound, saliva dripped from her lips.

I used the corner of her bedsheet to wipe her face and felt my eyes fill with tears and my chest tighten.

"Mom? Hey, mom? I...I need to go help with a cat for a day or two. Do you mind if I'm gone? I put food in the fridge, and we'll come check on you again, okay? Mom?"

I tried to keep my breathing steady and was about to turn away when I felt mom squeeze my hand again and I glanced back.

"Protect him," Renee said, barely a wilted whisper.

A little smile played on her lips and she released my hand. Her breathing steadied and I knew she'd fallen asleep.

"Yes, ma'am," Eiden said, equally quietly.

I leaned over and kissed mom on the head, tucking the blankets closer to her chest. I pushed a tiny sweaty curl from her forehead and realized I couldn't hold back real tears anymore so I turned and ran to the front door.

Eiden followed me and we both stopped on the porch as the door swung shut behind us, heavy and final.

I looked around at the broken wooden boards. I'd never realized how bad the porch looked. Hannah had a lot of thriving plants in her house.

Here, everything looked alone.

Forgotten.

Like me.

A hand squeezed my shoulder and looked up into Eiden's face. I was going to pull away from him but his sad expression stopped me.

"Sorry, kid. You're really brave," Eiden said.

I dropped my head against his waist and cried for a moment, his cotton shirt soaking up my tears.

"Come on, Lincoln. We need to go. I'll make sure Renee is safe, okay?"

I sniffed and nodded and we walked towards the car.

Hannah opened the back door for me and pulled me into a hug.

"You okay, buddy?" she said, pushing hair behind my ears.

"I grabbed this for you, before the bullets started, Hannah," I remembered. I reached under Juliet's cat carrier and handed Hannah a picture frame.

A smiling teenaged Hannah held a volleyball between two hands and on either side of her were two adults with proud expressions, their arms draped around her shoulders.

She reached towards the frame with her mouth open.

"It looks like the glass cracked, I'm so sorry, please don't be mad." I watched her face switch from surprise to sadness.

I should have protected the frame better when we were running.

"Lincoln. How did you think of grabbing this in all the chaos? I can't even tell you how much I appreciate this," Hannah said, her voice breaking.

Eiden adjusted the rearview mirror and his eyes were dark watching us. Jerry was silent in the front seat, his eyes wandering out the window.

“Are those your parents?” I asked. I’d never seen a picture like that other than in movies from many years ago. It looked fake.

Hannah nodded and sipped a breath.

“Where are they?” I added.

“They died when I was sixteen. Just a few months after this tournament,” Hannah said, her eyes glued to the photo. “Thank you, Lincoln.”

I glanced up at Eiden who reflected Hannah’s stilled moment. His eyes flickered above me, out the broken back window and he started the car.

"Not now, Hannah. Shit. Buckle up!"

CHAPTER TWENTY

HANNAH

"GO, EIDEN. GO!" I yelled as a black SUV nosed our bumper.

"What is happening?" Lincoln asked as the Cutlass Sierra lifted its nose and lurched forward like it enjoyed the chase.

"Probably the same people as earlier," I said, pretending I understood any of it.

"Who are they?"

"I don't know," I said with a sigh. "Eiden? Jerry? Now would be a good time to let me in on the secret everybody else seems to know."

"Yeah, me too!" Lincoln said, leaning forward.

I pulled him back against the seat as Eiden swerved around a corner, the tires screeching loudly. Jerry's knuckles whited on the handle above his head.

"I've seen you before, Eiden," Lincoln said as he resisted my hands and leaned towards the front seat. "And I don't mean at the hospital. You sat outside my house one night."

I watched Eiden's shoulders stiffen then soften. He tensed as he rounded another corner.

"Yeah," Eiden said sadly after straightening out the car.

"Mom was in the hospital for about a week," Lincoln continued. "But I had food in the fridge the whole time."

Lincoln reached down and straightened Juliet's carrier. He shoved his hair off his forehead, then rested his elbows on his legs and his chin in his hands.

"You put food in the fridge, didn't you?"

I met Eiden's eyes in the rearview mirror. He looked like he was battling a choice. He searched my eyes for a moment, then looked back to the front of the car and sighed.

"Yeah, kid, I did," Eiden admitted.

How long has Eiden been protecting Lincoln?

"Why did you do that?" I asked.

Lincoln glanced at me.

"I was hired to protect your mom," Eiden said.

Jerry glanced at Eiden, then over his shoulder at me like he already knew the answer.

"But she was in the hospital that week. If you were protecting her, why were you at the house?" Lincoln said, sitting up.

“You needed me more,” Eiden said quietly.

Eiden knew exactly what he was doing when he drove into that intersection. Lincoln may have spent a lot of time hungry and alone, but he was alive because of Eiden.

“Eiden! They’re gaining on us!” Jerry said. He scrunched himself deep into his chair.

I glanced behind us as the SUV found our bumper. Eiden turned suddenly and the SUV missed the turn.

“Take the skyway! You can get off at Outer Harbor and hide under the overpass!” I said pointing to the right.

"Watch out!" Jerry yelled as the SUV caught up again and shoved the Oldsmobile forward.

Lincoln leaned into me and allowed me to hold him. The lap belts and bench seating of the older vehicle didn't help much with stability.

"Hold on," Eiden said as he tore through the roundabout at Niagara Square. "Let's lose these morons."

"Do you have to drive so fast?" Jerry said, wringing his hands between clamping on the handle above his head.

Eiden drove left and right then ran a never-ending red light and rocketed up the ramp. The sedan groaned as we climbed the steel arch of the Skyway.

Lincoln looked up, curious but frightened.

I was glad there was nobody shooting guns.

"Just over the arch of the bridge, there's an exit. If you go fast enough, you should be able to ramp off the Skyway and turn left under the overpass." I said, hoping Eiden heard me over the noise of the wind.

For a split second, it felt like a movie—the kind where the good guys always get away from the bad guys. I glanced behind me and noticed our car was pulling ahead.

My idea might actually work!

The Oldsmobile took the final curve on the ramp deftly and arched over the peak of the overpass. The top-heavy SUV behind us was forced to slow down and I lost sight of it.

Eiden drove down the off ramp and turned left under the highway. He stopped suddenly and everybody lurched forward.

The only sound was the engine and Jerry's deep breathing.

"We need to get out of town," Eiden said, looking at the roof of the car as if it contained a blinking GPS dot of the SUV's location.

"Who is after us? Why does Leota care if I know Lincoln?" I asked again. "So he's Harold's nephew, what of it?"

"Uh, Hannah?" Lincoln said, tugging on my sleeve.

I heard a tapping on the window by my ear and glanced over to see a homeless man. He held a jagged piece of metal fashioned into a weapon against the window. A cruel smile played on his lips.

"Eiden?" I pushed Lincoln behind me and glanced at the door panel to make sure it was locked.

The man switched from tapping to hammering and then noticed the back window was missing. He stepped backwards and leaned his head over the trunk and grinned a toothless grin at me. He lifted his hand, his homemade weapon in the air.

"Eiden!"

The older man fell off the back of the trunk onto the street as Eiden lurched forward and turned left, ramping back towards the city.

"They're back!" Jerry said from the front seat, looking over his shoulder.

I heard squealing tires and knew the SUV figured out our maneuver. I glanced back and saw the man jump out of the way as a dark SUV sped under the bridge.

"SUV, incoming!" I said to Eiden who seemed very focused on the road in front of him. The snow had begun to fall in sheets, and temperatures were already causing slick spots.

Eiden maneuvered the long sedan back onto the skyway and turned on the wipers, the snow falling thick and blinding. He rounded the curve with only a little slip on the back end of the car.

“They’re falling behind,” I said, updating Eiden, who was leaning forward over the thin steering wheel.

“Here’s the plan,” Eiden said, angling the car through the curve on the exit to downtown.

He sounded like he should be asking for help instead of trying to sound confident. The moment of doubt in his voice made me feel less strong. I felt my hands begin to shake.

What if we don't get out of this?

"At the next intersection, I am going to stop in front of the museum," Eiden said after a bit. The strength in his voice had returned. "Go through the front door then exit through the south door, which is at the back of the building. You'll be in a narrow alley way."

"How do we get into the museum without a ticket?" Jerry asked as he buttoned his jacket.

Eiden ignored him with a shake of his head and continued directing.

"When I get there, you need to exit the car immediately and step back so I can leave. In the alley way, you'll find a small red door, get inside as fast as possible. The people chasing us don't care about your life. They will kill you if they find you."

The whole car fell silent. Even Jerry didn't have any more questions.

"Got it?" Eiden said, louder.

"Yes!" I said, although I'm not really sure I got it.

In my head, I echoed Jerry's question of getting through the museum, but I believed Eiden had some plan. I *needed* to believe him. I certainly didn't have any plans. I grabbed Juliet's carrier and looked over at Lincoln. He nodded at me and put his hand on the buckle release by his hip. I smiled confidently and held my breath.

"Now!" Eiden said as he rolled to a stop.

Three doors slammed and before I could release a breath, the car was gone.

Juliet and her carrier were wrapped in my left arm, Lincoln's hand tightly curled in my right hand.

Jerry grabbed my elbow and directed me up the stairs to the entrance of the museum, mumbling something about needing a ticket.

CHAPTER TWENTY-ONE

HANNAH

THE STEPS TO the museum felt longer than a climb in a coliseum. We were all breathing heavily when we crested the final step and ran to the grand entrance doors.

I heard a car squeal to a stop and a door slam. I knew someone had been dropped off at the bottom of the stairs, chasing us.

“Hurry!” I said pulling Lincoln faster. My heart was fluttering and I felt like a mouse in an open field with vultures circling above.

Except I didn’t even know who we were running from.

I felt Lincoln squeeze my hand and glanced over at him. He looked so calm as he held the front door open for Jerry and me.

Inside the door was a rope laid out in a zig zag pattern designed to hold long lines. Lincoln ducked under the ropes and approached a woman standing by a box taking tickets.

"Please take the appropriate path, young man," the woman called out pointing at Lincoln.

"Oh ma'am, I'm so sorry. See, we were here earlier, and I left my favorite stuffed animal by the back door. I can't go to bed without it, I really can't!" Lincoln said, as if it were the truth.

I stopped short behind Lincoln and tried not to show my surprise at his quick thinking. Juliet meowed from her carrier and the woman stepped around her podium.

"And, uh, we don't allow...cats inside," she added. She looked at my face, then Jerry's. "You guys okay?"

I decided against adding to Lincoln's story. I was certain whoever had been dropped off out front would be coming through the doors any second.

I glanced at her name tag.

"We just need to go through the back door to the alleyway, Shaquelle," I said, my voice begging.

"Please," Jerry squeaked. Juliet meowed again.

Lincoln grasped my hand as tight as he could.

"Follow me," Shaquelle said after a brief hesitation. Her black braided hair whipped around her shoulders as she turned around, her high heels clicking across the marble floor.

I choked back a sob of relief.

We ducked under the final rope and followed the woman into the first gallery.

I wanted to hug her—this stranger who decided, without knowing us, that we mattered.

Jerry grabbed my arm and tilted his head behind us. Reflected through a series of mirrors and glass walls behind us, I saw the outstretched arm of a man holding a gun.

"Go, Lincoln, we have to move faster!" I half-whispered while I hunched over, trying to make myself a smaller target.

Four rooms later, the woman pointed to an emergency exit door.

"Thank you, I hope we didn't put you in danger," I said, touching the woman's shoulder.

She smiled and held up a black walkie talkie in her hand. Her thumb was hard pressed on a red button.

"I'll be fine," she said but her voice was drowned out by shouting.

"Put it down!" I heard behind us as we ran out the back door. "On the ground!"

The heavy metal door latched behind us and Shaquelle yelled something about this area being clear.

"The door!" Jerry said pointing to a faded red door, about two feet wide and two feet tall. He crossed the alley and turned the handle, the door groaned as it swung inwards.

"Get in!"

Jerry dove in, followed by Lincoln. The dark space swallowed them up and I tried to pretend I didn't feel like I could have a panic attack in the inky nothing in front of me.

"Hannah!" Lincoln called.

I dropped to my knees, shoved Juliet's carrier in, and crawled through the door frame. I fell on top of someone, I think it was Jerry, then slammed the door.

"Ssh!" Jerry said and I heard a metal lock slide into place.

A loud engine approached and we all moved backwards until our backs were flat against a cool, stone wall.

Lincoln wrapped his arms around me and I put my hand on his back. I could hear every piece of gravel crunch under the slow-moving tires until it stopped in front of the red door.

"I swear I saw them in this alley."

I knew that voice. My hands began to sweat.

The door handle jiggled but caught against the slide bolt.

My breath caught in my throat and I felt Lincoln stiffen.

"That's just an old coal chute, probably been sealed up from the inside for decades," a deeper voice said, almost bored.

Someone kicked the outside of the door and tried the handle again.

"If your goon hadn't pulled his gun, maybe we would've been able to stop them," the familiar voice snapped.

"He's an idiot, sure, but they're going to run until we stop them. This is your fault and you know that." He paused. "Whatever happens next is on you."

I looked toward the sound of Jerry's stilted breathing, but couldn't see him. I felt his nerves—sharp, specific, certain. He knew what I knew.

"Why would they run into an alley? That side is blocked, and we were on the other end."

"They can't get far on foot."

A police siren sounded in the distance.

"Let's get out of here."

A car door shut.

"Dammit!" The man said, kicking the door again.

After a few more moments, a second car door shut and tires squealed. The engine sound dissipated as the police sirens grew closer.

"Did you hear that, Hannah?" Jerry said, letting out a long breath.

"Yeah...yeah, I did," I said, even though I didn't want to admit it out loud.

"What about it?" Lincoln said, shifting on the floor.

"Argh!" Jerry cried as a single light bulb turned on and broke through the endless dark.

I blinked a few times and pulled Lincoln closer. Jerry rubbed his eyes then stared at me blankly. Neither of us knew what to do.

The square room was barely wide enough to fit us side by side. The wall behind us was mostly stone and the doorway to the alley was positioned near our feet.

Suddenly the wall we leaned on opened up and Lincoln and I fell onto our backs.

Lincoln whimpered, and I stared up into the dark eyes of the deli owner's evil wife.

CHAPTER TWENTY-TWO

LINCOLN

"DELI DEVIL!" I jumped up and threw my hands into the air. "I'm sorry, I'm sorry. I didn't know this was your place. I will leave right now—just tell me where the door is," I said, looking around desperately for an escape.

Why is she here?

"Lincoln, shh, it's okay," Hannah said standing up. She put her arm around me. I could feel the Deli Devil's eyes boring into my soul. I refused to look at her but I stopped trying to find the exit and leaned into Hannah.

"Follow me. Hurry," Deli Devil said quietly. She turned and walked down a narrow, dimly lit hallway.

Hannah looked down at me just as confused as I was. I'd never heard Deli Devil speak softly. Her tone was always sharp and cutting.

Jerry crawled out of the room through the small doorway. He brushed off his pants and walked after the woman.

"Come on, guys!" he said hurriedly, like this had been the plan all along.

I heard Hannah take a deep breath. She grabbed my hand and nodded firmly. We both followed Jerry through two hallways, then up a narrow set of wooden stairs. I could smell sugar in the air, and suddenly I was thinking about donuts.

"How did we get in the deli?" I asked, perplexed.

Hannah stepped aside to let me climb the stairs in front of her. I took the stairs two at a time.

"The museum and the building the deli is in back up to each other in that alleyway. I never realized the owners lived behind the storefront, though," Hannah explained.

At the top of the stairs, Deli Devil grabbed a string in the ceiling and a small set of stairs opened and touched the floor by her feet.

"Go up there. Stay quiet until I return," she said.

Jerry nodded and climbed the creaky wooden ladder until he disappeared into the ceiling.

"Lincoln, go ahead—but be careful," Hannah said as she followed me into the attic.

We sat in a row on the floor, with our backs against a huge wooden beam that spanned the entire length of the unfinished attic space.

Nobody said anything. Even Juliet was quiet. I think we were all wondering what to do next. I was tired and hungry. And the attic was cold. I scooted closer to Hannah and she put her arm around me, warming me immediately.

The big fan on the wall made a humming sound that reminded me of the train tracks that ran by my house and I imagined how good my bed would feel right now.

I let my eyes close and drifted off to sleep.

CHAPTER TWENTY-THREE

HANNAH

LINCOLN'S BREATHING WAS steady and calm. The kid never complained. The moment his head settled on my lap, he was asleep.

Was it still Friday? The only reason I'd kept going all day was pure adrenaline. Sitting on the attic floor, I didn't feel like the adrenaline would wear off anytime soon.

I reached my hand into Juliet's carrier and gave her some neck scratches. She began purring instantly. She didn't have a litter box or food, but she seemed to have decided it was a good place for a nap.

I needed a phone.

"I accidentally found out what Harold did," Jerry said, interrupting my thoughts.

"What did he do?" I tried not to sound impatient, but I was strung tight. I didn't feel any choice I made right now would matter because I didn't understand anything.

"I approached Harold, telling him I suspected, but he ignored me—so I told the feds about the things I'd seen in the books," Jerry said, stumbling around his words.

"What kind of things?" I questioned. Based on our work relationship, I knew Jerry would eventually get to a point. But I really needed him to walk me to that moment faster because my hands were beginning to sweat.

"Shipments. Things that shouldn't be shipped, especially over the border," Jerry said after a moment.

The attic fan suddenly roared to life behind me.

"Illegal stuff?" I asked.

"Yeah. I decided to tell him I knew, that I was going to report him..."

"In the office?" I interjected, but Jerry kept rambling. As if he'd finally decided to bare his soul to a priest in a booth.

"...And there was a gun sitting on his desk. He said, if you know what I did, then shoot me. I deserve it," Jerry lowered his voice and I leaned closer to hear him. "He did deserve it, Hannah. But I couldn't do it. So I came out into the office floor to tell everybody else...and...the gun went off."

I felt myself shrink back against the wooden beam and my chest tightened like I'd missed a step on the stairs. I could still hear the bullet hit the ceiling as if it the gun had just been fired. The sound of the police officers yelling and Jerry shouting, crumpled underneath four burly men, still echoed in my ears.

My jaw locked.

"I didn't mean it..." Jerry rushed on. "I didn't know it was loaded. Never held a gun before. Only did it like I'd seen in movies. Thought I'd just get everybody's attention. Wanted people to know that they were working for a fraud. He did bad things. And we could all be liable."

Jerry turned towards me and gripped my arm, then looked at his hand and dropped it to his lap.

"I didn't want to hurt anybody," Jerry said glancing up at the ceiling. He paused and I worked so hard to stay quiet. "But the cops were there, Hannah. *They were right there*. The second the gun went off, they were on me."

"I never thought about that, but you're right," I said, unable to stay quiet any longer. A cold chill settled between my shoulders. "It was immediately after the gun went off. And why did Harold have a loaded gun on the desk?"

I pictured Harold pacing his office and glancing at his desk periodically, knowing Jerry was coming. Then making a rash decision, he peered out the office door and settled the gun on the desk, making sure to load a bullet. He'd worked with Jerry for fourteen years, knew how Jerry handled confrontation, and how he thought.

He probably counted on Jerry never telling federal agents about his crimes.

“I didn’t go to jail. The police officers took me to the county jail, but then the feds picked me up and took me to a different office where they gave me coffee.”

“Everybody thought you went to jail,” I said, mostly to myself. Then I remembered nobody talked about Jerry once he left. I’d just assumed everybody thought that.

Unlike me, everybody moved on. Everybody healed.

"I told the feds what I'd found and asked to be left alone, said I didn't want a part in anything. I didn't think he'd come after me," Jerry added.

"You were offered witness protection?" I said, mentally sitting in the office, watching it all unfold again.

"They seemed to already know about the shipments."

The shipments. Harold and Leota. Protecting their illegal income. Jerry found out.

My hands were unsteady as I reached out and squeezed Jerry's shoulder. I tried to see the human in front of me, not the wild man waving a loaded gun.

“I’m so sorry you were in that alone,” I said. “I wish I had known the truth. Is that what you wanted to tell me on Sunday at the tournament?”

“I wanted to protect you from Harold,” Jerry replied reaching out to absently fidget with Lincoln’s blonde curls. “To tell you to leave and never look back.”

“But now...” I said, glancing down at Lincoln who twitched in a dream, his breathing steady.

I wanted to ask more questions, but Jerry was already somewhere else—lost in a narrow alley of thought, Lincoln’s curls his anchor.

I understood some of this mess now—but not the part that mattered.

Jerry's finger stilled in Lincoln's hair as if he heard my thoughts.

The room felt different with Lincoln asleep on my lap, like my vision had narrowed around him. Everything else—that attic, Jerry, the story—fell slightly out of focus. I could follow the danger until it reached Lincoln. Then it vanished, like a cut wire.

"That burly guy who chased us in the alley isn't office security," Jerry said. "He works for Harold. I survived by disappearing. Now it's your turn."

I opened my mouth to argue, then stopped.

I looked down at Lincoln, and the dream I'd been pulled out of that morning flickered back—not images, but in sensation. The attic fan spun by us, replacing the waves, the panic eased into something steadier and I felt my chest loosen.

Fear didn't get to make the next decision.

"I can't sit around and pretend nothing happened anymore," I said, meeting Jerry's eyes.

I didn't fear what Jerry did.

I was afraid of the silence after.

CHAPTER TWENTY-FOUR

LINCOLN

I WASN'T SURE how long I'd slept, but I was startled out of a dream about a yelling caterpillar and a barking dog.

Hannah and Jerry were watching the hole in the attic where we'd climbed up the narrow stairs. Loud voices echoed through the walls.

Hannah felt me sit up and put a finger to her lips, telling me to stay quiet. I nodded and listened, trying to figure out why the voices were so angry.

"What are you hiding?"

"We've kept your secret, what else do you want?" A man replied.

"Whatever you've gotten yourself into now, that's on you," a woman's voice added.

"You'll regret this!"

I put my head back against Hannah and she wrapped her arm around me.

"Oh yeah, like the last seven years haven't been enough?" the woman said, her pitch heightened.

"Shut up, lady!"

I clamped my lips together and pushed my head against Hannah as glass shattered and the woman screamed.

Hannah put both her arms around me and her forehead against my hair. I tried not to cry. I hope the woman wasn't hurt, but she sounded very scared.

Two doors slammed, one after another, and then the floor below us was silent.

Jerry had his head in his hands and was rocking forward and back, quietly muttering to himself.

Hannah noticed and reached her hand out to Jerry.

"It's over, Jerry," Hannah said.

A tap on glass a few feet from us startled us.

Hannah released her hands from around me. Jerry stood up too fast, hitting his head on the ceiling. I expected him to swear, but he just pressed his palm on the cut and ducked back down on his heels.

I was afraid to look over at the window.

"Eiden!" Hannah said in a half-whisper.

I looked up and saw Eiden outside the window in a pose like a cat, with his knuckle against the glass.

"I'll let him in!" I said. I needed to move. I was stiff and bored. Hearing all those angry voices made me feel restless.

“Lincoln!” Hannah said, reaching after me, but I’d already walked several feet across the wooden beam and she couldn’t catch me. “Be careful!” she added, barely above a whisper.

The window was shaped like a stop sign and had several pieces of paneled glass. The middle one was about the size of a large dog and had a latch that slid to the side easily.

After the latch slid free, I pushed the glass outward. Eiden folded himself through the opening, shoulders first, careful and quiet, like he’d practiced it—twisting until his boots cleared the frame.

“Everybody okay?” he asked.

I nodded and pointed to Hannah and Jerry.

Jerry lifted his hand a little above his knee and waved. Juliet meowed and Hannah stared, her mouth slightly open.

We froze when the attic ladder groaned and dropped a few inches on its chain, the sound loud against the quiet.

I thought about jumping out of the window Eiden had just crawled through when I heard a voice that made me feel like I was about to watch my favorite movie.

"You all want some food?" the voice said.

I looked at Jerry. His arms were crossed and his fists stuffed inside his sleeves. Hannah had her arm on Jerry's, like she was using him as a brace.

Eiden walked towards the opening as if rehearsed. He stopped and looked at each of us.

"It's okay, guys," he said with a little chuckle.

Nobody said anything, but we went down the narrow staircase one at a time.

The man at the bottom put his warm hand on my shoulder, then turned me in front of him and propelled me forward. I looked back at Eiden but he just nodded and continued to follow him.

I could smell the sweet smells of the deli again and wondered if we were going out the front door. I wasn't ready to leave, yet. I was hungry and it had to be near midnight. Where would I go? I didn't want to walk back to my house. My bed would be very cold.

We didn't go to the front door. Instead, we went to the back of the building that looked like a living room. Two green couches flanked an old television. A lamp in the corner glowed yellow against the ceiling.

A glass coffee table had several sandwiches, croissants, and various Danishes arranged on gold plates. A stack of paper plates and little cups were placed carefully on a corner table.

My stomach growled but I wasn't sure this food was for us. Deli Devil could have put it out here just to torture us before she shoved us out the back door into the alley.

“I’m sorry you got dragged into this,” Deli Devil said to Hannah.

I stepped behind Hannah and pretended I didn’t exist. I wasn’t sure if she’d seen me yet.

The woman exhaled, slow and heavy, like she’d been holding her breath for hours. “I don’t mean you any harm, Lincoln.”

Her voice was softer, but still distant. I didn’t believe her.

“There’s a long history between your uncle and us. Longer than you could remember. I kept my distance on purpose. I needed you to stay away from me. From this place."

I peeked around Hannah's waist and saw the woman gesture at the wall.

"I thought if you hated me, you'd stay safe. I kept my distance because that was the only thing that ever worked."

She looked at Hannah, then over at the man in the doorway. Something sharp and yet apologetic crossed her face. "Until it didn't. I can't undo that now. And I can't protect Lincoln the way I once thought I could. I've already lost too much."

She straightened, as if remembering herself.

“I’m Rhonda, and this is my husband, Irving. Please, eat. But be quick. You can’t stay here very long.” Rhonda squeezed her hands together and looked at the various foods she’d placed on the tables.

Hannah gently grabbed my hand and led me to the food. I glanced up at her face and she smiled.

“It’s okay, really. It’s been a long day. We all need food,” Hannah said. “And you know this is going to be the best, too, coming from the Huron Street Deli.”

“Thank you,” Jerry said, one sandwich already inhaled and another in his hand.

Well, Jerry wasn’t dead yet, so maybe Deli Devil wasn’t trying to kill us or kick us out. My stomach growled so loud that Hannah giggled.

I glared at her then grabbed a plate and filled it with one sandwich and two treats. I picked a wooden arm chair in the corner and listened to the adults talk.

"We have to find a way to expose Harold, and stop Leota," Hannah said between bites. "I imagine he wants to keep himself from going to jail, but would he really kill us?"

"Yes," Eiden said. He'd chosen a Danish and only taken a small bite so far.

"Sure, these shipments are illegal, but is that worth offing everybody that finds out?" Jerry added, reaching for his third sandwich.

"It's not just the shipments," Rhonda said sadly. She handed Hannah two bowls—one with plain shredded chicken, and one with water.

Hannah smiled at her and crouched down to put the bowls in Juliet's carrier.

Perhaps Rhonda isn't so bad after all.

I was feeling pretty good after eating some food, but then I looked at Eiden's face. His lips were in a hard line, like he wanted to speak but nobody would believe him. Hannah didn't seem to notice so I didn't say anything.

"Then what is it?" Hannah said, standing.

"I...I don't really know too much," Rhonda said. She looked nervously at

Irving, who sat silent in the corner opposite me. "Seven years ago, something happened with Harold and he dragged us into it."

"What do you know that can help us?" Hannah said.

"I...I can't say anymore. You all need to leave, and take care of Lincoln. He doesn't deserve the childhood he's been handed. I'll get boxes for the rest of the food. I'm...I'm sorry," Rhonda said. She turned on her heel and left the room.

I looked over at Eiden. He was leaning back against the wall by the door to the hallway. His eyebrows were scrunched and he was watching Hannah intently.

"We can't just hide forever," Hannah said, throwing her hands in the air. "Whoever is chasing us clearly has endless bad guys and they blew up my apartment! I deserve to know who is doing this and why!"

Eiden smiled at Hannah's outburst.

"Lucy! My best friend is a computer genius, maybe she can find information."

"We don't need to endanger anybody else, Hannah," Eiden said, his mouth a straight line again.

"I'm done staying silent, Eiden! After Jerry's event in the office, everybody existed like nothing had ever happened, and I was expected to do the same. I'm done! Sorry, Jerry."

Jerry swiped at the air and went back to eating.

"All safe places are known by Harold's guys at this point."

"I don't use social media and I wasn't a threat until today. They probably found my home address through office records, but likely don't know much else about me yet. Even if they had tapped my phone, it's long gone."

I suddenly realized I'd eaten too much sugar and was getting very sleepy.

"Can I go home and sleep now?" I said with a yawn.

"Jerry—do you still have contact with the feds who gave you coffee?" Hannah asked.

Eiden glanced over at me then at Hannah, his eyebrows creased.

"Somewhere, I'm sure," Jerry replied.

"You go find them, be safe. Let them know what's going on. See if they have a way out for us. Does anybody have a cell phone?" Hannah said.

"I picked one up," Eiden said, reaching in his pocket. He handed her a small grey rectangle.

That doesn't look like a real phone. Why is it so small?

"I know a place in the Southtowns that is boarded up for the winter," Hannah said while typing on the phone. She paused then smiled. "It'll be ready when we get there. Let's sleep then decide tomorrow what to do."

Rhonda finished packing the food in containers and handed me a grocery bag. She smiled at me and I decided to smile back. She looked like she might cry.

"You're dealing with dangerous people, please be careful."

"I'll bring Jerry wherever he needs to go," Irving said using his hands on his legs to help him stand. "I have deliveries to make in one hour, my normal routine. He can hide in the back."

Jerry and Irving left the room and Hannah, Eiden, and I were led to a back door that opened into the alley by the red door.

"Where's the Oldsmobile?" Hannah said, stopping in the doorway.

"I left it in a scrapyard and borrowed a different vehicle," Eiden replied, pointing to a black SUV with dark windows.

"You *borrowed* a Range Rover?"

"Cool!" I said racing to the passenger door. "Can I sit up front?"

"No, you're not tall enough. Pennsylvania plates? I'm not getting in a stolen vehicle," Hannah said crossing her arms.

"Fine, I'll sit in the back like a president being escorted in a parade," I said and opened the back door.

Eiden chuckled.

"Hannah, it's not a stolen vehicle; it's a company vehicle. Get in," Eiden said.

I couldn't hear Hannah's response, but she climbed into the front seat and shut the door.

I buckled and snuggled into the soft leather seat and began poking buttons on the screen in front of me. I really did feel like a president. This seat was way better than the front.

"Where am I going?" Eiden said, starting the vehicle.

"Angola-on-the-Lake. Third exit off Route 5."

CHAPTER TWENTY-FIVE

HANNAH

WE WERE MOSTLY silent as we drove south. The near-blizzard weather required Eiden to move slowly, but I never felt nervous or scared by his driving.

By the time we neared our exit, the tires were barely moving, and it was a struggle to see anything in front of the car. We slid past the exit and had to back up. Eiden deftly maneuvered the SUV in the intersection and righted our course.

Approaching Lake Erie, I barely recognized an area I knew so well. For a week, the weather reports had warned of lake effect snow coming, but it hadn't meant anything to me until now.

"We may get snowed in," I said to no one in particular. "Wonder if Harold knows how to drive in the snow."

Eiden snorted and I realized I was overtired and talking just to talk.

I glanced out the window to entertain myself and the snow lifted enough I spotted Tasty Freeze, a local ice cream shop, boarded up and covered in snow. If someone didn't know what the business was, they certainly wouldn't know now.

I shivered and Eiden glanced over at me.

"How much further?"

"About four streets, then you'll cross a bridge. Pull into the first driveway on the right. There are three houses on the driveway, we're the one closest to the water."

"Whose house is it?"

"My aunt's house," I said, turning away. "She and my uncle go to Florida during the winter."

We approached the bridge and crept across. I pointed to the driveway and saw Ben's sedan parked on the street. Always careful, Ben probably didn't want to get stuck in the driveway. Eiden sped up and plowed to the end of the driveway, parking next to a bungalow-style home with a porch over the sand. Large windows opened towards the lake for endless views.

Ben opened the side door to the house, stuffing his hands into puffy coat sleeves and holding another.

"Lincoln. Lincoln? We're here buddy," I said, trying to see into the dark backseat.

I heard him mumble something in response.

Eiden watched Ben walk around to my side of the car. I saw him grimace as Ben opened my door.

“Hannah, are you okay?” Ben asked, reaching his hand up to me.

“Yeah, I’m fine,” I replied tiredly allowing him to help me out of the tall SUV.

“Who is that?” Ben asked, handing me the extra coat.

“Let’s just get inside, Ben,” I said handing him Juliet’s carrier.

Ben took the carrier with a surprised expression and I reached around him to open the back door. Lincoln stepped down and I put the coat around his shoulders.

Ben stared at the kid and I realized I'd forgotten to tell Lucy I had a second grader in tow.

"Hannah!" Lucy said waving from the door, her feet bare. Her hand froze mid-wave as Eiden jumped down from the driver's side.

We all went inside, kicking snow from our shoes.

Ben opened the cat carrier and Juliet scampered upstairs.

"I put the litter box up there already," Lucy said as she handed blankets to each of us. She kept glancing over at Eiden then at me.

"Thank you, Lucy. Juliet's been in that carrier for hours."

I knew she was dying to make a joke about something romantic about Eiden and I silently begged her to save it for now.

In the living room, I sank into the couch and Lincoln climbed up next to me.

"Lincoln, Ben, Lucy, Eiden," I said, pointing to each person.

Eiden nodded at Lucy and I thought she might faint. Ben and Eiden stared at each other.

"We brought a space heater. Fortunately the electricity is still on," Lucy rambled, staring at Eiden. "The water is off, so use the toilets wisely. I put a few things in the fridge for you."

If I wasn't so tired, I'd probably have teased her about the silly grin on her face. But I didn't know how long my eyes could remain open and I certainly wasn't in the mood.

"Ben, can you get that heater set up in here?" Lucy said.

Ben broke his glare to Eiden and followed his sister to the kitchen.

"Are you sure we can trust him?" Eiden said to me. "I don't like him."

Despite my exhaustion, I smiled.

"He's my brother, you moron."

Eiden's mouth opened then shut again.

I felt bad not giving him more information, but I wasn't required to, and

I wasn't even sure I could formulate the words.

Lucy and Ben returned with a large grated box and set it down by the wood fireplace. I longed for a roaring log fire, but a smoke signal would be a bad idea right now.

Ben plugged in the heater and Lucy turned the dials on the front. Within moments, the warmth breaking through the icy air was noticeable.

"Wi-Fi is no good, Hannah. It's been broken for months, but mom refuses to fix it. Says 'we're at the beach, why do we need internet?'"

I smiled picturing Lucy's mom, Vivian, worrying herself over internet. She could have lived her whole life without technology and been perfectly content.

Lucy asked Lincoln to help her set up the blow up mattresses and spread the blankets. Lincoln jumped up and grabbed a blanket, excited to have something to do.

"Guess we'll reschedule our date, Hannah," Ben said as he adjusted the angle of the space heater.

I looked over at him, his face smug. He glanced from me back to Eiden.

"Ben, give it a rest," Lucy said over her shoulder as she and Lincoln smoothed a blanket over one bed. She looked at me apologetically. "Help us finish the beds?"

I rarely got mad at Ben, usually just annoyed, but I knew what he was doing, and I didn't appreciate it. Boys could be so ridiculous.

I stood up to help Lucy and glanced over at Eiden. He was looking at me with the most confused look and for a moment I wanted to tell everybody to just leave me alone. I was tired of explaining. I was tired of thinking. I was…tired.

"I can stay to make sure you're safe," Ben said as he walked over to me and helped straighten a comforter.

"No," I said and heard Eiden echo my word. "I'm okay, really. It's been a long, weird day, and I will be asleep within a few moments."

"I'm done!" Lincoln said brightly from the third bed as he carefully placed another pillow.

"Good work, Lincoln," Lucy said kindly. "Thank you for your help. You're very good at making beds."

Ben looked crestfallen but I told myself it wasn't my responsibility to fix it.

"Here is a basic cell phone for everybody," Lucy said, holding out three boxes. "They've just been activated. Each of our numbers are programmed into the phone book."

"I get one, too?" Lincoln said, reaching his hands out, a disbelief in his tone.

"Sure! You're a man, Lincoln," Lucy said as she crouched down and helped him unbox his phone.

A man too soon.

Eiden seemed to echo my sentiment, a sad smile on the corner of his lips. He caught me looking at him and I turned away.

Lincoln beamed up at Lucy. She pulled the corner of the bedding down on the bed closest to the couch and patted the pillow. He crawled into the bed and I was certain he was instantly asleep. Lucy tucked the blankets around his chin and pushed soft curls off his forehead.

"I can't work here without internet," Lucy said standing up to face me. "I got what you sent, and I will stay up all night if I must to figure out what's going on. Is there anything else you need?"

She hugged me tight.

"No, thank you. For everything. Down to the litter box."

"Happy birthday," she whispered quietly in my ear and I felt tears creep to the corners of my eyes.

I'd forgotten for a moment.

I'm twenty-one, I realized.

She squeezed my shoulders and pulled her brother to the exit.

Ben waved a quick goodbye to me and glared at Eiden again. The door shut and I heard the car start at the end of the driveway and pull away.

I sat down on the couch and leaned my head back, forcing myself to focus on just getting some sleep. It didn't matter if it was my birthday. It didn't matter if we were running for our lives. Sleep mattered now.

"Incest is not legal in the state of New York," Eiden said.

I opened my eyes to see him standing above me with his arms crossed. I stood and looked up at him, barely holding myself together.

"They're my *adopted* brother and sister. Not that it's any of your business," I said. I walked away and took a deep breath. "Aunt Viv took me in when I was sixteen. Ben and Lucy were adopted when they were toddlers. I've known them nearly our whole life."

I heard Eiden let out a deep breath and the couch creaked.

"The picture frame Lincoln took from your apartment," Eiden said quietly, his voice deep and thoughtful, "those were your parents. What happened to them?"

I turned around and looked at Lincoln. He was twitching in a dream and content. Eiden's leg was crossed over his knee and his arm rested against the edge of the couch.

I was so tired I didn't know how much longer I could stay standing. I walked to the makeshift bed near Lincoln and sat down on the edge.

I rubbed my face then glanced up at Eiden. He was silent and unmoving, waiting. I really didn't want to talk anymore, but something about his expression opened a cavern in me and I fell into it.

"We were at a high school volleyball tournament in Albany where I lived. This was the kind of tournament where agents watch you. I'd just been told I received a full scholarship to University of Nebraska and wanted to stay after to celebrate with my friends. My parents arranged my ride back and headed home. But they never made it. Aunt Viv adopted me and I had to come to Buffalo to live. I finished high school here," I said, feeling empty. I laid down on the bed and looked up at the ceiling as the silence settled around me. I didn't need Eiden to respond, but I was curious what he was thinking. I traced the lines of the cracks in the ceiling above me and tried to stay awake. I heard the couch creak again and the sounds of the rubbery scuffing of a blow-up bed.

"I work for a private security company based in Pennsylvania," Eiden began. I turned my head to see he'd settled in a bed, his head propped up on his hand, watching me. "Seven years ago, I was hired by a client to watch Renee, to protect her. For one year, I watched her life away, but wasn't allowed to do anything other than make sure she didn't kill herself. Then suddenly, the contract was terminated and I was told to stay away. I fought with my boss over Lincoln so many times, but my boss—Charlie—man, she can be tough. Contract terminated, association done. She reminded me I can't get involved in something outside my scope," Eiden stopped. He stared at me for a moment, like he was deciding what else to tell. I watched him struggle with his choice and realized the man may be rude and crass, but he was still a human. I felt a sadness drifting from him. A regret.

"I never told her but I came to check on Lincoln periodically. Made sure he had food. One time found Renee overdosing and took her to the hospital while Lincoln was at school. I never...I couldn't...I felt like a god from the underworld, watching and doing nothing. Watching his sadness, his loneliness," Eiden's voice broke and he stopped talking.

"You saved him from being run over! He knew it was you from his mom's hospital visit. Lincoln will always remember the good you did, Eiden. And it sounds like you did a lot of it within the constraints of your job; that's all you can do," I said. I felt myself drifting off to sleep and settled my head back onto the pillow. "Thank you for telling me."

I heard Eiden adjust on the mattress and soon the room was silent. Juliet stepped across the mattress and settled by my hips, a soft purr rolled through the bed.

I don't know how long I slept, but my phone sounded rudely through my dream and Lincoln looked over at me from his bed, sleep still deep in his eyes.

Eiden threw off the covers and walked out of the room. Light pushed through the windows and I figured it was close to eight in the morning.

I grabbed the phone from under my pillow and blinked, squinting to read the tiny screen. It was a text from Lucy.

CALL ME ASAP...IT'S BAD

Eiden leaned against the doorway with a towel in his hands. I looked up at him and he nodded.

"Tell me," he said.

CHAPTER TWENTY-SIX

LINCOLN

THE NOISE FROM a cell phone woke me up. I yawned. I really needed more sleep. I listened to Hannah and Eiden talk for a few minutes about meeting someone later because they didn't want to discuss things over the phone. I decided I was done sleeping when my stomach started to growl. I threw off the blanket and looked toward the kitchen where Eiden stood at the stove.

"I miss my mom," I said.

Hannah walked around the corner and put her hands on her hips.

"Hey, pal. Did you sleep alright? We have some eggs and toast ready for you. Will you come sit at the table?"

I nodded and pulled my socks on. The air wasn't as cold as last night but my toes were still unhappy. I sat in the chair closest to Hannah and looked down at my plate.

Scrambled eggs, cheese, and buttered toast.

I hadn't seen a meal like this in years.

I almost didn't want to eat it because it was so perfect.

I glanced up at Eiden.

"Are you a superhero?" I asked.

Eiden snorted and turned away. "No."

Hannah put her arm around the back of my chair.

"Because superheroes don't get paid, right?"

He glanced over his shoulder at me. "Perhaps."

"Yeah," I said picking up my fork. "My comic books say they just show up when you need it."

Hannah sucked in a breath and Eiden was quiet.

"You showed up, both of you," I said with my mouth full of eggs. The texture melted in my mouth, and I wanted to eat fourteen pounds more. "Mom eats at weird times. Do you think she ate the food we left yesterday? We should probably bring her more."

"Yeah," Eiden responded. "We should."

Eiden walked over and set his plate on the table. Sitting down, he looked at Hannah. "But this time, we leave the cat."

I thought Hannah might get mad at that comment because she loved her cat, but she laughed instead. I smiled as I finished my food then put my plate in the sink.

"It's kind of a long drive to Niagara Falls, Lincoln. Why don't you watch something on the screen?" Hannah said once we all settled in the cozy car.

I knew that sentence. It meant the adults had something they wanted to talk about without the kid listening.

I pressed a few buttons on the screen in front of me. It started playing a show that I was too old for, but it was something to look at while I secretly listened.

Hannah and Eiden talked about meeting that nice blonde lady from last night, the one that said I was good at making the bed. I was excited to maybe see her again. I eventually got lost in a show about cats and superheroes and forgotten I was trying to listen.

"We have a problem," Eiden said loudly and I leaned over to look out the front window.

"Mom!" I cried, wrestling with my buckle.

"No, Lincoln, no!" Hannah said.

I opened the car door and ran towards the front of my house. A man had his arms around my mom's waist. She was kicking and hitting him, but he didn't seem to notice. Two more men were running up the driveway to help him.

"Mom!" I said again and then stopped. The men stopped, too. They looked over at me then back at the man holding my mom.

I knew then I'd made a bad decision. I thought about running back to Eiden. And Hannah. They'd fight for me.

But maybe they'd get hurt.

Right now, it was my turn to protect Mom.

I knew they'd find me later.

They were superheroes.

"Let my mom go!" I said, running towards the two men.

"Lincoln, go, no ... Lincoln! Don't touch my son!" I heard my mom say as the two men grabbed me and dragged me to their dark SUV. They shoved me in the back seat by another man.

I heard another door behind me shut and my mom sputtered words that didn't make sense. I heard the men ask where I came from but I ignored them and peeked over the back seat. Mom had her wrists and ankles tied and was lying on the third row. She seemed like she might have fallen asleep already.

"Sit down, boy!" a man said, and I obeyed. I looked forward and thought that this back seat was really uncomfortable compared to Eiden's SUV.

I leaned harder against the seat as the driver stepped on the gas and the tires squealed against the ice. The back end of the car drifted to the side and we didn't move.

"Idiot, get us back alive!" said the man next to me.

"Shut up!" the driver snapped. He let off the gas and slowly inched us forward until the vehicle gained traction then stepped on it.

"Where are we going?" I asked, trying to pretend I wasn't scared.

I'm not *scared,* I tried to convince myself. *I'm protecting my mom. This is what men do.*

But my hands were shaking.

And I didn't feel like a man at all.

CHAPTER TWENTY-SEVEN

HANNAH

"EIDEN!" I LUNGED for the door handle.

"No, Hannah. Stay in the car!" His hand closed around my arm.

"I can't," I said.

"There's nothing we can do right now. With weather like this, we'd only put Lincoln at more risk if we chased them.

We will find him." Eiden kept his hand on my arm, not viciously, but comforting.

The SUV in front of Lincoln's house struggled in the icy conditions, but eventually drove off.

"So unfair," I said, putting my other hand on Eiden's arm, trying to find my grounding and focus on breathing. "We shouldn't have brought him here. That son of a bitch is going to pay!"

I hit the dashboard and my hand stung.

I was done with hiding. Done with being chased.

"I don't care who is listening. Lucy can tell me what she found."

I dialed Lucy on the burner phone and she answered immediately.

"Things have changed. Tell me everything now."

Eiden pointed at his ear, so I switched to speakerphone.

"It's bad," Lucy said, sucking in a breath. "The Delaware Park Gang lost a family member to an overdose years ago. After that, they shut down their chop shop and started selling antiques. The feds haven't been able to pin anything on them since."

"Get to it, Lucy. What does this have to do with anything?" I felt momentarily guilty for snapping, but Lucy came right back.

"The gang is believed to be shipping their wares through a local company called Janeris International."

I nearly dropped the phone.

Jerry was right.

Illegal shipments.

Through our company.

Through Harold.

From a gang.

And Harold tried to bury it.

That's why the feds were involved.

"Did you find anything about what Harold has to do with it? Why are they using Janeris International?"

"I'll keep looking," Lucy said, and disconnected.

"This shit ends today! I must find Harold's address. If he's wrapped himself up in some stupid gang stuff, this shouldn't affect Renee and Lincoln! But maybe he'll know where they are and we can get the police involved."

"What are you going to do, walk up to his house and point your finger at him?" Eiden said, pulling the car forward. "He's protected himself this long, to the point where he has his goons after you."

I didn't have an answer. So I ignored him.

"I can call our office manager, Debbi. Maybe she'll give me his address. She knows something, too. She knew Lincoln."

I dialed Debbi and let it ring until the voicemail answered.

I ended the call, frustrated and fuming. I rolled down the window and sucked in the frigid air.

How do I find Harold?

My phone dinged and I opened a text from an unknown number.

OFFICE

"Go to my office, Eiden," I said without thinking. "That intersection where you saved Lincoln's life. But park on the south side of the building. Nobody can see that area from inside."

"Who was the text from?"

"I don't know. But if it gives us Lincoln back, it's worth following."

"They tried to kill you four different ways yesterday. Why do you want to save Lincoln? Go get your cat. Save yourself," Eiden said, staring me down.

"Why did you still protect Lincoln when you were no longer 'employed' by the security contract?" I shot back.

"Because somebody had to." Eiden looked away.

"Yes, you keep saying that...but nobody required you to. Nobody asked you to," I responded.

"His mom got into drugs because of Harold. That wasn't Lincoln's fault."

"What did Harold do?"

"I'm not entirely sure I even know. He's the one that hired me to protect

Renee and he's the one that canceled the contract."

"If you're going to continue protecting Lincoln, so am I. After all, you told me to protect him."

"Fine."

"Fine." I crossed my arms.

After a brief hesitation, Eiden put the car in drive and carefully maneuvered through the snow-packed streets.

I stared out the window and waited for the response.

The sweaty hands.

The mind battles.

The shaking.

None of that happened.

I know what the danger is.

The danger is in Mr. Leota's unnerving presence, Harold's callousness, and Debbi's sweeping-everything-under-the-rug attitude.

I am no longer silent, and I'm demanding the same of everybody else.

Eiden coughed, and I realized we'd already parked.

"You sure this is what you want to do?" he asked.

His eyes were soft, his lips in a slight frown.

"Are you worried about me?" I asked, then instantly regretted it. Despite the danger around us, I felt myself blush.

"Nah, I'm afraid of you, too," Eiden said smiling now.

He turned to exit the vehicle and I was grateful he didn't linger on my stupid line or make fun of me.

We traipsed through the snow to the front door where I entered my pin. Eiden pushed the door open and held it for me.

The lobby lights were on, which was unusual for a weekend. The building felt occupied but the security desk was empty.

I walked quickly to the elevator, not feeling much. I couldn't tell if I was fueled by adrenaline, fear, or just numb enough to float outside my body.

I reached out to press the elevator call button when Eiden grabbed my wrist.

"Wait, let's take the stairs," he said, nodding towards the door to the left. "It's safer."

"Oh yeah, let's corner ourselves in a stairwell instead of an elevator. That really makes a difference," I said, rolling my eyes.

Eiden smiled as he headed to the stairs and I told myself to save the sassy remarks for Harold.

"Sixth floor," I said, following Eiden.

We climbed in silence, trying to step lightly. I tried to rehearse in my head what I would say to Harold, but I figured in the moment I'd forget everything anyways, so I gave up trying.

On the last turn of the stairwell, I glanced up to see the large number six hanging above the doorframe. I felt my lower back tightening and knew I was afraid now. I took a deep breath and climbed the last few steps.

“This ends today,” I said, and this time Eiden chuckled out loud.

CHAPTER TWENTY-EIGHT

LINCOLN

THE SUV DROVE for what felt like hours. I bet I could have driven better. The SUV scraped several curbs and multiple cars, like it was on ice skates. The man to my right yelled at the driver and the driver shouted back.

"She needs to be buckled!" I demanded as we cornered abruptly and my mom slid across the back seat.

"I need to buckle her!" I said, nearly panicking.

"Alright, alright, kid!" the man to my left said. I unbuckled and tried to crawl over the back seat.

"NO!"

I felt a cold hand grab my ankle, and I froze mid-climb.

"Shut up, like for real. Where's he gonna go?"

The hand let go, and I fell to the floor in front of Mom.

I heard a man chuckle but I scrambled onto my feet quickly.

I reached up and pulled the seatbelt down from the roof. I heard a click, and knew she was secure. I cradled Mom's head on my lap and buckled myself.

"It's okay, Mom. I've got you."

I heard one of them mutter something about withdrawals. That she'd probably die anyway.

I pretended I didn't hear him say she'd die. I found her hand and squeezed it.

"I won't let you die," I whispered to her.

I felt tears touch my eyes when she squeezed my hand back.

The men argued over different topics for the last part of the drive. I tried to keep track of where we were by looking out the window, but the buildings zoomed by too fast.

We came to a stop near a large tan building with missing windows. The air smelled like toasted oat rings cereal. I wondered if Mom had eaten today.

“Don’t touch her!” I said as the back of the car opened and beefy hands reached for my mom.

I tried to yell at him again, but it didn’t matter.

Nobody was listening to me.

The man sitting on my right brought his head down to my level.

“You do what we say, or your mom dies. Got it?” His eyes were red. His breath smelled like dog poop.

I nodded and he slid out of the car. Cold hands grabbed me and yanked me out into the snow. He kept one fist locked around me and dragged me forward.

I walked as quickly as I could after him. The wind pushed snow around my ankles, trying to swallow my legs. After a few steps, I finally saw Mom by the door. I pulled back against the hand.

"Please, she needs to eat," I begged, trying to lean closer to my mom. I couldn't tell if she was trying to say something or just drooling in her sleep.

"Your mom doesn't know up from down, idiot. She'll be fine," said the stinky breath guy and he grabbed my other arm. He chuckled. "Or she won't."

"Shut up, moron," said cold hand man to stinky breath guy. He pulled me closer to him and picked me up over a snow drift taller than my head.

I looked up as he walked us through the entrance of an old warehouse. A golden cross hung above a large staircase. The cold hand man set me down and pointed up the stairs then began climbing. I glanced behind me and saw the man carrying my mom following.

Keep going, I said to myself.

I shuddered against the cold.

Superheroes don't stop at the bottom of the stairs.

I put my foot on the first step.

CHAPTER TWENTY-NINE

HANNAH

I APPROACHED THE door at the sixth floor landing and reached out.

“Hannah, wait,” Eiden said, touching my shoulder. I turned around and looked up at his face.

“I’m going to stay here,” Eiden said. He stared down at my face, his expression unreadable.

"Oh, okay," I said. I felt deflated, like my forward momentum was suddenly blocked.

I don't need him to take care of this mess, I lied to myself. *He's the ace in my pocket, not my bulletproof vest.*

"I'll be here if you need me," he said, walking down a few steps.

I nodded at him and grabbed the door handle. I believed him.

The office floor was dark, the cubicles towered in the shadows. A light spilled on the floor from the open door of the conference room by the elevators.

I walked across the blue carpet squares, as I had many times before.

I stopped under the door frame and blinked.

Debbi, Harold, and Mr. Leota stared back at me. My confidence wavered as I tried to judge everybody's need to be in the same space at the same time.

"Shut the door," Harold barked.

"No, thanks," I responded. I leaned against the door frame and thought of Eiden in the stairwell eavesdropping.

I've survived bullets and a car chase. I can survive a conference room.

"Don't be naive, Hannah. You know better than most that things can change in one innocent moment," Mr. Leota responded with a sneer.

"You summoned me?" I said, this time directed at Debbi. I tried to sound strong, but instead sounded more cliché.

Mr. Leota grinned.

Debbi frowned. I barely recognized her. Her usual forward mannerisms, waiting for the next juicy gossip, were nowhere to be seen. She leaned back deep in the chair, her expression vacant, somewhere else.

"I want nothing to do with whatever is happening, but apparently I'm somehow involved now," I risked a glance over to Leota, who had a glorified smirk settled on his lips. "Can someone please tell me what is going on and how do I get out of it?"

I decided then not to admit I knew Lincoln.

Harold and Leota exchanged looks. Then they both looked at Debbi. Debbi looked down at her lap. I imagined she was wringing her hands beneath the table.

"You helped a man yesterday. Pulled him from a car wreck," Leota said, taunting. "We need him."

I decided to play dumb. He'd clearly seen enough to know some of the truth.

"Yeah, that wreck was awful. He was unconscious and bleeding. I've never seen anything like that in my life. Why do you want to find him? I'm assuming he's at one of the local hospitals?"

"You were at the hospital," Leota responded, planting both feet firmly on the ground. "You know about this already."

Debbi bristled and looked like she might cry. Her eyes pleaded with me, a story I couldn't define.

"At the hospital? Yesterday? When would I have time for that?"

Debbi leaned forward.

Leota took two steps towards me and pointed at my face.

"You didn't deliver the mail until 3:45 PM. You always deliver it at 11:29 AM, right before your lunch. What were you doing?"

I tried not to gulp, and looked over at Harold. His hands were clasped tightly behind his back and his lips were a straight line. He refused to meet my eyes.

"Harold," I said, lowering my voice. "Call off your dog. He's barking up the wrong tree."

"Call me a dog again," Leota said quietly, closing the distance between us. I could smell his clothes—a birch mixed with cheap beer.

Debbi stood up and slammed her hands on the table.

"You've tortured enough souls. Leave her alone!" She yelled.

"You want to test that theory, bitch?" Leota said, his breath hot on my face.

I told myself to remain steady. To wait.

A door slamming echoed through the vacant floor and Leota whipped his head around.

He put his arm on my shoulder and shoved me roughly to the side. Stopping for a moment, he said over his shoulder, "Nobody leaves."

Leota stomped off into the darkness and I subconsciously willed for Eiden to run and hide.

I turned around and quietly shut the door between the office floor and the conference room, not entirely sure what my intentions were.

"Hannah," Harold said, louder than expected and I spun around. "I know you're a good, sweet kid. And you're a valuable employee. I don't want anything to change. But, you've seen things, and, it's a bad place for you."

"Is that a threat? You're talking to me like I'm eight years old," I responded in hushed whispers.

Debbi lowered herself back to the chair and set her face in her hands.

"No...maybe a warning," Harold stammered.

I was beginning to feel that deep desire to speak up. To be heard. Like I was being told to be silent again.

"What is your goal, here, Harold?" I said and bristled.

I'd never called him by his first name before and he noticed. He turned his back to me.

"I want it the way it was before."

"Before what? Before Jerry?"

I felt like I was pushing him too far; being too harsh. Like this wasn't my place.

He chased me into an alley. His nephew is missing. And somehow I'm the one who is fighting to protect Lincoln.

I looked over at Debbi, hoping she would back me up. But she shook her head. I shook my head back at her, trying to tell her I won't be silenced anymore.

"Jerry?" Harold said, his voice faded into a distant memory. "Oh. Jerry. No."

"What happened, Harold?" I was trying not to freak out and barely containing my patience. "What did you do, Harold?"

"Hannah, stop," Debbi said sharply. Her fingers gripped the edge of the table.

"It wasn't my fault! I want it to go back to before he died."

"Before *he* died? Who died!"

"Hannah!" Debbi said again.

"My sister couldn't handle it," Harold interrupted. "She turned to drugs."

I ignored Debbi's hands waving at me to stop and walked over to Harold. I put my hands on his shoulders and forced him to face me.

I wondered where Leota was, and if he'd found Eiden.

"Yes, Renee is an addict. But Lincoln is a child. You turned your back on him! How could you do that to your own family?"

"You don't know what you're talking about, Hannah!" Debbi said, her voice cracking.

"Then what *should* I talk about?" I said, releasing Harold. "You're in your posh office taking limos to fancy dinners with a bodyguard while Lincoln is starving and running around the streets of downtown Buffalo alone. Meanwhile,

Renee is holed up at home with her next fix and off in la la land."

Or in a ditch somewhere...

I paced to the end of the table and ran my fingers through my hair. I tried to push the image of Lincoln alone somewhere, crying for help.

"We made an... agreement," Harold said after a moment. "Renee and I, after the... event. After John died, Renee blamed me. She said I wasn't allowed to see Lincoln anymore. I hired someone to watch out for Renee, quietly. I don't know when she started taking drugs. The guy watched her for a while, but eventually refused after she got so deep in her own shit."

Eiden wouldn't do that, wouldn't say that.

"You're lying," I said.

Harold threw his hands up in the air and stepped left then right. His voice grew louder.

"If John hadn't died, none of this would have happened! I've been paying for it ever since. Renee wouldn't be a useless mother, and her son would be thriving."

"Hey, she's not a useless mother," I snapped. "She's sick! And apparently your life choices put her there! And guess what?"

Lincoln alone. His mother beyond help.

I choked back a sob and my voice broke.

"Someone kidnapped Lincoln and Renee, Harold. *They have Lincoln.*"

Debbi's mouth dropped open. Harold turned red and whipped around to face me.

"Are you sure?"

I nodded and Harold wiped his hands across his face like he could wipe away the guilt that settled behind his eyes.

"Your bodyguard already does your dirty work," I said. "If anyone knows who you pissed off enough to kidnap your sister, it's him. We need his help to get Lincoln back."

Harold stomped over and Debbi's breath caught.

"I need that man!" Harold said through his teeth, his finger nearly pressed against my nose. "The one you pulled from the car. He's the only one who can save us!"

"Save us from *what*?" I asked.

I heard the metallic click before I saw the door opening.

CHAPTER THIRTY

LINCOLN

MOM HAD BEEN mumbling a lot. When we first got here, I sat close to her, hoping we could keep each other warm. Then she started wandering around the room, talking to something I couldn't see.

I was beginning to shiver when she stumbled over to me and fell on her side.

"Need more. Get me more," she said, her head turning side to side.

She screeched and reached her hands toward the ceiling, like she thought it might fall on her.

I tried to scoot away from her but she grabbed my ankle.

"Mom, I can't get you anything right now," I said, frightened. I'd never seen her like this.

"Ask, ask them. They know. They know what I want," she said, her hand pointing at the stone walls.

She released my ankle and mumbled something about rain on the birds.

Obeying, I knocked on the wooden door.

"Excuse me, sirs? Mom is asking for her medicine," I said.

The only response was a chuckle, and goosebumps climbed up my back.

I tried to ignore the chill and knocked again.

"She's really sick, sir. Do you have her medicine?" I said louder.

"Your mom is a drug addict, idiot. No medicine will help her," the voice with the bad breath said with a sharp laugh.

"Dude, stop calling the kid an idiot," the other man said.

"Yeah, 'cause it makes such a difference. We can kidnap him, but I'm not allowed to call him an idiot? Moron."

"Shut up."

I heard a chair move across the stone floor.

"Lincoln, Lincoln," I heard Mom say. I turned around to see her trying to get up off the floor. Her whole body was shaking. After one step, she collapsed onto the dirty, grey floor.

"Guys, she's shaking really bad. She can't get up."

I ran over to her and saw white foam form around her mouth.

"Help! Mom!"

"Open the door," the man said.

"No, she can die."

I tried to hold Mom's head up, but she was shaking so bad and rolling her head back and forth I couldn't steady her.

"If she dies here, we die, too. You know that. Open the damn door!"

The chair scraped the floor again and keys rattled.

The two men rushed in.

I tried again to lift her head off the cold floor. Tears were falling on her forehead.

"Mom, Mom. Mom you can't die!"

"You brought me a druggie without drugs. She's going through withdrawal. If she dies, it's not on me," the guy yelled into a phone.

"Get off her, kid," the man said, grabbing my shoulders.

I thought he was going to shove me away, but he didn't let go.

The guy shoved his phone in his pocket and grabbed Mom off the floor. Turning towards the door, Mom's head hit the wall and she went limp.

"No, Mom! Where are you taking her? Mom! Wake up! Let me go!" I yelled, kicking at the man.

His hands tightened on me, and he squatted to the floor. Turning me around, I smelled cold air and gasoline.

"You'll live," he muttered. "It doesn't kill you. Feels like it does. But it don't."

I didn't know if that was true.

But I stopped fighting.

My face fell against his chest, and he held on.

CHAPTER THIRTY-ONE

HANNAH

LEOTA STEPPED INSIDE and shut the door behind him. He raised the gun at me, a sneer settling onto his lips.

His phone buzzed. He glanced at the screen, then answered without lowering the gun.

"Yeah."

His eyes locked on mine as he listened.

"We have a problem," he said finally, shifting the gun toward Harold. "Your idiot sister tried to die."

Debbi went rigid. I sucked in a breath.

"She dies when I say she dies."

Harold put his hands up.

"I didn't change the agreement! I'm here. What do you want?"

I glanced over at Debbi. Her shoulders were straight, lips pressed tight.

"Agreement?" Leota laughed once. "You mean allowance. We *allowed* you to stay alive. Her and the kid. Lincoln, isn't it?"

"No, no, no. I did what you asked!" Harold said, nearly sobbing. He wasn't arguing anymore. He was pleading.

"John was reckless! It wasn't my fault he died! I'll pay. I'll fix it."

Leota snorted.

The barrel swung back to me.

"Hannah," he said. "The man asked you a question."

I bristled. I heard Debbi do the same.

"Where is Eiden?"

My mouth went dry.

CHAPTER THIRTY-TWO

HANNAH

I JUMPED AS the door exploded inward. The handle punched a hole in the drywall, then bounced off.

Leota whipped around, raising the gun higher.

Eiden jumped from the doorway and smacked Leota's hands. The gun vaulted over the men and slid across the table like a hockey puck.

Debbi screamed and fell to the floor, her hands over her head.

Leota shoved Eiden into the doorway and wrapped a hand around his neck.

Eiden dropped, twisting free of Leota's grip.

He ducked and wrapped his hands around Leota's waist, sending him stumbling backwards.

Harold narrowly jumped out of the way and looked over at the door.

My legs locked as I watched the two wrestle.

I glanced at the gun, only a step and a reach away.

Did I even know how to fire a gun? Would it matter?

"Where is Lincoln?!" Eiden yelled.

"You," Harold breathed, bracing his hands behind his back. "You were the one I hired."

Eiden landed a punch on Leota's face, and he stumbled backwards.

"Leota has been blackmailing me!" Harold shouted.

"Shut up, you idiot!" Leota grunted, his back to me.

Leota's arm arched back, preparing for impact, and I took that step forward.

I landed stomach-first on the table and stretched my fingers toward the gun, but I was short.

I heard a commotion behind me. Thick fingers wrapped through my hair and arched me back, tossing me to the floor. I landed hard on my hip and looked up to see Leota gather the gun, his finger sliding onto the trigger.

I glanced over at Eiden and caught his eye. He was breathing heavily, but his eyes were soft, like he knew what was about to happen.

No.

The sound of the gun cracked the room in half and the lights flickered. Eiden jerked backward, crashing into the wall.

Not again, I whimpered.

Time slowed and the floor tilted up to me. I put my hands out and let my head fall to the carpet squares.

I will not be silent, I said through deep breaths.

I dragged my fingernails across the carpet and balled my fist.

I sat up.

Eiden hadn't moved. He faced away from me on the ground, one arm twisted underneath him.

Leota had Harold by the shirt sleeves.

The gun pressed into his temple.

"If you want your sister alive, you come quietly," he said.

CHAPTER THIRTY-THREE

LINCOLN

I STOPPED CRYING after a few minutes.

I didn't move for a long time.

Neither did the man.

I wasn't shivering anymore.

He didn't say anything else. That was okay with me. I didn't have any words, either.

We both startled when a car engine echoed through the stone walls. The man lifted me and gently set me in the corner.

He turned toward the door, then hesitated for a second.

I looked down at my feet.

The heavy door closed with a bass-filled thud, and I was alone.

The cold wrapped around me like it'd been waiting.

I scooted into the corner and wrapped my arms around myself, wondering how to survive the quiet.

I didn't have to figure it out, because several men started shouting. Car doors slammed. Heavy footsteps approached.

The yelling turned into angry, clipped sentences.

"Open the door," a deep voice commanded.

I heard a woman's voice speak a sharp word.

It sounded familiar.

It sounded like...

My stomach flip-flopped.

My prison door swung open.

Hannah and a red-headed woman were shoved inside. The woman tripped and cried out.

Righting herself, she looked up at me and stopped.

Hannah stumbled in but caught herself on the wall. She brushed herself off, then turned around.

Her eyes found mine and her shoulders dropped.

"Lincoln!" Her voice broke. "You're okay!"

She held her arms out.

I ran and threw myself at her. She staggered backward, but I didn't let go. I wrapped around her and held on as tight as I could.

Maybe if I clung tight enough, we'd both be safe.

CHAPTER THIRTY-FOUR

HANNAH

LINCOLN HADN'T LEFT my arms. He wasn't sleeping—his fingers fidgeted at the end of my sweater like he needed proof I was still there.

The stone room was cold. I clung to the warmth of Lincoln against me.

Men's voices drifted in from somewhere down the hall. Metal clanged and doors slammed. With each crack, I saw Eiden fall again.

"Are you okay?" I asked Debbi, trying to avoid the silence that was beginning to swallow me.

Debbi nodded and shifted her hips, her short arms crossing and uncrossing.

Despite the chill in the room, Debbi's forehead was slick with sweat.

"They didn't bring Harold in here," Debbi muttered, her voice shaking.

I scanned the room.

I couldn't decide if that was safer or a bad sign.

"Did you hear anything about Renee?" I asked quietly. I felt Lincoln twitch.

Debbi shook her head. "It was just a lot of shouting. I hope Harold is okay."

I nodded and we were both silent.

"So, you knew about Harold and the FBI?"

"I heard enough conversations. I pieced it together I suppose," Debbi said, shrugging her shoulders.

"Did you help silence Jerry?" I said.

Lincoln glanced up at me then buried his head again in my shoulder.

"No! I would never," Debbi blurted.

"Then why didn't you say anything?"

"I had no choice!" she said, taking a deep breath. She whispered, "They threatened my job."

"Your *job*?" I said, bewildered. I didn't know if Eiden was bleeding out on the conference room floor—and Debbi was worried about her job.

"It's all I have, Hannah," Debbi said, looking down at her knees. She brushed a speck off her pants, then crossed her fingers.

"Someone's life is on the line because you were scared to lose a paycheck?" I knew my words were too harsh when her head snapped back up and she stared at me, her expression clouded. I took a deep breath.

"*My* life is on the line. You think I stay because it's perfect? I stay because I don't get second chances. If I lose this job...I disappear."

"Debbi...this job can't be the only thing you are," I wasn't sure if I felt pity or irritation. I tried to understand better. "Jobs aren't what save us, people are."

"I have no kids and no pets. At Janeris International, I'm important. I'm necessary. I feel like I exist," Debbi said.

She wasn't whining, she wasn't complaining, just stating a fact like it had been written in a history book.

"Debbi...we don't know what the company will look like after this," I gestured around. "Jobs can't save us. They don't hold our hands. They don't come looking for us if we've gone missing. It's what we have outside of those walls that makes us real."

I felt a pang of guilt. I was lecturing her about home, and I didn't even have one anymore.

I have siblings, I reminded myself. I wondered if Lucy had found more information. My burner phone had been abandoned in the conference room.

Eiden. I hope you're okay.

I glanced at Debbi, her head against the cold stone. My stomach knotted at the thought of being truly alone. Who was I to judge her? I had a cat, family, and friends.

"Once I figure out my apartment situation, how about you come over for dinner sometime?" I said. I wanted to add "if we get out of this mess" but cut myself off.

Debbi lifted her head and smiled at me. Not the smile she used when she was about to leak a juicy rumor. A genuine smile.

Lincoln stirred again and sat up.

"Hey, kid," I said, rubbing his shoulder. "You warm enough?"

Lincoln nodded.

"I have to use the bathroom," he said. He looked desperate.

"So do I," Debbi added, raising her palm.

"That's not a bad idea, actually," I said, a plan forming in my head. "We can use the bathroom in turns. Look around. Count people. Count voices and doors. Don't stare, just notice."

Lincoln stood up and bobbed his head.

"You okay with that, Lincoln?"

"I'm eight. I'm not a baby." He planted his hands on his hips.

"Yes, you are. A big kid! Debbi?"

She nodded. I stood up next to Lincoln.

If we were going to survive this, we needed information—and we'd have to find it ourselves. I fought the urge to wrap Lincoln back into my arms. If they separated us again, I wasn't sure I'd get him back.

I swallowed the panic and forced my hands to be steady.

I knocked on the door.

"Sir? We need to use the restroom. Can we please take turns or something?"

I heard a muted conversation.

Everybody held their breath as the handle turned.

Lincoln's hand tightened on my sleeve.

I wasn't sure if I'd made a plan—or a mortal mistake.

CHAPTER THIRTY-FIVE

LINCOLN

THE MAN PEEKED his head through the door. His eyes moved between the three of us.

"Kid. You first," he said.

Hannah stared at me like she might follow me, but she didn't.

I turned sideways to get through the door, then looked up at the man.

He pointed to an unsmiling guy I hadn't seen before in an oversized coat and black hat.

I followed the new guy for a few steps, then glanced back at the man. He nodded and shooed me forward.

Keep track of what you see, I remembered, echoing Hannah. I continued on my path. The overhead lights flickered. I could see my breath puffing in clouds from my mouth.

Two men so far. One sort of okay one, and one I don't know.

Several doors, all closed.

I tried to keep count but gave up.

Hallway is really long. Too many doors.

And it smells like dog food.

No windows on this end.

The door we came in from is way behind me.

I heard talking, but I didn't know from where. It echoed too much in here.

Footsteps crossed overhead.

A voice said, "We're still waiting on him. Two minutes."

The guy pointed to a door, then pulled on black gloves.

Behind the door I found a toilet with brown water and a leaky faucet. I used the toilet as fast as I could. I touched the water in the sink to wash my hands, but decided it was too cold. I promised myself I'd wash once I warmed up.

I pulled open the door. The hinges creaked and the guy jumped up from a blue chair. He grabbed my shoulder and jerked me back against the wall outside the door. He stood tall and nodded as two young burly men in brown jackets rushed by. They were followed closely by a bald older man in a white coat. The bald man stared straight ahead and didn't look at me. He talked in hushed tones to the two men. They reached the end of the hallway and pushed open a door. A dirty metal staircase gleamed in the overhead lighting and the men disappeared as the door slammed behind them.

The gloved hands turned me back toward the stone room and pushed me ahead.

The man saw us approaching and opened the door. I squeezed back through.

"You next," he said, pointing to Debbi.

Holding the door open wider, Debbi exited.

The door closed and the lock clicked.

I turned around and grabbed Hannah's hands. I tried to remember everything I had seen.

"There are a lot of people," I said, trying to catch my breath. I was beginning to shiver again. "Two men outside our door. More upstairs. I saw three men walk by. One had a white coat, like doctors wear. They went up the stairs. The hallway is really long."

"Did anybody say anything to you?" Hannah asked.

"No, even the man with the hat didn't talk," I said.

"I'm so glad you're back. Oh! You're shivering!" Hannah said sitting on the ground. She pulled me onto her lap and put her arms around me.

I leaned into her embrace and tried to still my chattering.

"You did a great job, Lincoln," Hannah said into my hair.

I smiled.

I *did* do a good job.

CHAPTER THIRTY-SIX

HANNAH

THE DOOR OPENED wide and Debbi returned to her spot against the wall inside the room. She rubbed her hands together.

“Get up,” the man said from the doorway.

I patted Lincoln on the back and pointed to Debbi.

“Keep him warm,” I said.

Debbi nodded and pulled Lincoln into her coat.

The man closed the door behind me and sat down in a blue plastic chair.

“He’s freezing,” I said over my shoulder as a gloved hand pulled on my elbow. “You could at least give him a blanket.”

Several closed doors were set into walls covered in graffiti and cracked stone. The air felt colder than my freezer and smelled of dog food and pine needles.

No wonder Lincoln came back shaking. I have to find a way out of here. We can’t stay in this cold for long.

We stopped in front of a door and the gloved man reached for the handle, then froze. He turned around and shoved me behind him.

I heard booted footsteps and leaned around the man's large coat to see.

Three men hurried by, one in a white coat. His eyes caught mine and a look of recognition crossed his face. He reached up to his chest and flipped a badge over, but not before I saw the crest of the hospital Lincoln and I had snuck into the night before. He frowned but kept pace with the other two men.

Is he here because of Renee?

After they'd left through the main door, the man opened the door behind us and shoved me in.

The smell was overpowering. Under the flicker of a single bulb, I glanced at the toilet, brown with age and use. A calcium covered faucet dripped into a green and yellow sink. I tried to tell myself it was better than nothing and at least there was toilet paper.

I flushed and waited for a moment to leave. I replayed what I'd seen in the hallway, and begged my mind to turn it into something useful.

A shout and a crash made me jump.

Lincoln!

I opened the door and peered around.

The gloved man was running toward the front entrance where one other man was wrestling with someone. The heavy doors were open and snow blew in.

"You said you wouldn't hurt her! Where is she?!"

Harold punched a man, and another tried to grab his wrists. Harold slipped out of his hands and took two steps my direction.

He paused. I couldn't tell if he was looking at me or the gloved man running towards him.

"Take me to her!" he yelled, without breaking his stare.

He turned on his heel and ran through a door. The three men dove in after him.

I bolted from the bathroom directly across the hall and threw the door open.

I needed to find a phone or a weapon to hide on me before the man came back.

Broken wooden crates littered the floor and art-covered boxes filled the corners. I backed up and tried another door.

Locked.

Harold yelled again and I heard a crash.

One more door then back to the bathroom, I decided. I opened the door at the end of the hall and found a poorly-lit staircase.

A figure stepped out of the shadows.

I nearly screamed.

"Jerry?!"

"Door," he whispered. "Now."

I shut the door as the yelling and banging continued.

"I can't leave Lincoln!"

"We'll get him soon," he said, and began climbing the stairs.

"We?"

"Upstairs. Hurry!"

I looked once toward the hallway where Lincoln waited.

Forgive me.

Then I followed Jerry up the stairs.

CHAPTER THIRTY-SEVEN

LINCOLN

DEBBI WAS WARMER than Hannah, but she held me stiff, like she wasn't used to holding kids.

"Do you have kids, Debbi?" I asked. I was comfortable, but my stomach was starting to complain.

"No. Just... never worked out for me," she said. She sighed, her breath warm against my hair.

"Are you too old now?"

She laughed softly. "Maybe. I don't know."

She sounded sad, but also like she was smiling.

At home I'd watch a movie to forget I was hungry. But Debbi felt more interesting than a screen.

"I like your red curls," I said. "Do you really only like your job? Nothing else? I like flowers. Have you ever planted a garden?"

Her chuckle turned into a real laugh before she coughed.

"I like your blonde curls," she said, messing up my hair. "I like flowers, too. But no. I've never planted any."

"Maybe I can teach you," I offered, even though I didn't know how.

"That'd be fun. I'd like that," she said. "Thank you."

I thought about what she'd said earlier. About disappearing.

"You won't, you know," I said.

"Won't what," she asked.

"Disappear. Not if you don't want to."

She took a sharp breath and went still.

"You're worth it," I added. "Thanks for keeping me warm."

Her arms tightened around me and I hugged her back. She didn't feel awkward anymore.

The door slammed open.

Cold air rushed in.

The gloved man stormed in, eyes frantic.

"Where is she?!" he barked.

Hannah left?

"If she's not here," I shouted back, "she's saving my mom!"

Then I buried my face in Debbi's jacket and held on for whatever came next.

CHAPTER THIRTY-EIGHT

HANNAH

JERRY OPENED THE door from the stairwell to the next floor. I glanced left and right and followed him. He seemed to know where he was going, like he'd been here before. He looked at his hand before every move, and I realized ink lines were drawn across his palm.

"Jerry, where are we going?"

I ran into his back when he stopped suddenly. I looked around him and saw a man. He was the one that'd been guarding our cell. He glanced at us then turned away. He scratched the back of his head with one finger, then ran his fingers through his hair. Jerry and I stood frozen in our spot as the man once again scratched the back of his head with his finger flat.

"He's pointing, Jerry!" I whispered. "The door, there!"

The man started shouting at something we couldn't see. I grabbed Jerry's arm and ran through the door marked with a number two above the frame. Voices grew louder as we dove behind a large, plastic-wrapped crate, labeled “JANERIS INTERNATIONAL – FRAGILE” in large lettering.

From a reflection in the window, I saw the same hospital worker walk in with Leota and Harold. The man who guarded my cell brought up the rear. He looked around anxiously then seemed satisfied and settled into his job of protecting the door.

In my haste to find a hiding spot, I hadn’t noticed an occupied hospital bed in the middle of the room. I looked over at Jerry and he looked at me with surprise.

Renee? I mouthed and Jerry shrugged.

"Doctor Hoc, will she be okay?" Harold said, his voice shaking. His cheek was bleeding and one eye was swollen shut.

"She's rough, but she's alive. For now," the man in the white coat said, glancing down. "You can expect violent shaking, paranoia, nausea. She might even beg for you to let her die," Doctor Hoc said like he'd said it a hundred times.

I heard plastic ripping and the doctor set a tray of needles by Renee's feet. I couldn't see her face, but I didn't see any movement. Perhaps she'd already been given something to help with her withdrawal.

Leota grabbed Harold's arm and pulled him close to the pallet where I hid.

"You tried to play both sides," Leota said, his voice controlled. "That's not how this works."

"I didn't do it," Harold pleaded. "I didn't do it."

"You tell us who else knows and we'll think about saving her."

"No! I don't know anything. I told you what I know!"

"You hired an out of town private security team," Leota pressed. "Did you think we wouldn't notice?"

Harold leaned into Leota's hand and pulled at his fingers.

"It was brief, I didn't know what was happening and I wanted to protect my sister. I cancelled them as soon as I knew you were upholding your side of the deal. I trust you!"

"Trust me?" Leota sneered. "You've got that Hannah girl doing research on us."

Renee sat up and screamed. Her arms flailed, sending the tray of needles flying off the bed. Doctor Hoc drove a needle in her arm. She fell back and the whole bed began to shake. Harold and Leota stared at her. After a moment her shaking settled. The doctor gathered the scattered vials and placed them back on the tray.

He checked her pulse and nodded at Leota.

"She's stable. For now," he said.

Harold looked helplessly at his sister.

“What did you give her, Doc?”

“Clonidine, anti-nausea, and some sleeping meds,” Doc said flatly. “She already had a stabilizing dose.”

“You’re…you’re giving her drugs—on purpose?”

“Weaning her off is a better way to state it,” Doc said. He looked tired and ready to be anywhere but here.

Harold looked over at Leota, his lips twitching. His expression flip-flopped between fear and anger.

“I’ve never told Hannah anything. That accident was your fault!” Harold stepped closer to Leota. “She never would have known Lincoln existed if it wasn’t for your idiot goons trying to run down my nephew!"

Harold rolled his shoulders back then they sagged forward and his head dropped.

Leota's phone rang. He grinned at Harold then answered. He nodded to the door guard and they both left the room.

Doctor Hoc watched the men leave, then turned to Harold, unsure what to do.

"Is she in pain?" Harold asked, approaching the bed.

"She'll stabilize for a few hours," Doc said with relief. "After that, it gets ugly again. It's going to be hell for her."

Harold's shoulder sagged and he reached for his sister's hand.

"Get her to a medical rehab facility as soon as you can," Doc whispered tiredly.

Doctor Hoc gathered his instruments and packed them into his medical bag. He nodded at Harold then left the room.

Jerry poked me and gave me a thumbs up.

I stood up and gasped when I caught sight of Renee. Her face was pale. Her skin barely covering her bones. Her eyes flickered about but her body was still. She looked bad when I had knocked on her door—was that yesterday? But now she looked like a clay figure that hadn't yet hardened. I tore my eyes away and walked around the crate.

"Who is really in charge, Harold?" I said.

Harold whipped around, his hands scrunched up against his chest.

"Why are you still here?" he said breathlessly. "I created a diversion for you!"

"I won't leave Lincoln," I said.

"Where is he?" Harold said.

"In a cold, dark cell. With Debbi."

"Oh, oh. What have I become?" Harold ran his fingers over his face.

I heard plastic shudder and watched Jerry climb out from behind the pallet. He tripped over the corner. Righting himself he stood up and walked over to Harold.

Harold stepped around Renee's bed and watched Jerry as he approached. Harold's eyes were large and his lips tight. Jerry seemed so calm. So certain.

"You set me up, Harold," Jerry said. He pulled on his shirt and looked away.

"I...I didn't have a choice," Harold whined.

"You always have a choice," Jerry responded with conviction. "This is the part where you fix it."

CHAPTER THIRTY-NINE

LINCOLN

A THUD SHOOK the door and Debbi and I jumped. We looked at each other as if we held the answers.

Metallic scraping—like keys on iron—dragged across the lock then fell to the floor.

I stood up and clenched my fists. I hoped maybe Hannah was coming back.

Otherwise it would be the guy, and he'd torture us to find her.

My heart pounded in my ears as the lock clicked and the door swung inward.

Eiden peered around the corner and my fists opened.

I grabbed onto his coat to make sure he was real. I wanted to cry but I didn't.

"You came," I said.

Eiden nodded once. "Yeah, kid."

He looked relieved to see me, too.

I let go of his coat and pointed behind me.

"This is Debbi," I said sniffling, "She works with Hannah. She's the big boss lady."

Debbi smiled and they exchanged nods.

"You work with Hannah? Is she here?"

"Yes," I said, nodding. "There were two guards in front of our door and Hannah, she was so brave. She came up with a plan for us to each take a breath to go to the bathroom. But really, we were just looking around. Hannah didn't come back after her break, and the guard was really mad."

"That was very brave of you, Lincoln," he said, then paused. He rustled my hair and looked around.

"Debbi," Eiden said, glancing behind him. "If I get you to the exit, can you go get help?"

"Yes," Debbi said, rolling onto her knees. "I think so."

She stood up and walked closer to me. She put her hands on my shoulders and squeezed.

"Alright then, let's get you guys out of here," Eiden said turning towards the hallway. "I found a safe place for you, Lincoln."

I stepped backward, deeper into the stone room.

"No," I said crossing my arms. "I won't leave without Hannah and my mom."

Eiden stepped over to me and wrapped his hand around my arm.

"I need to protect you, first. Then I can come back for Hannah and your mom."

"I'm not leaving!" I said and shook his hand off me.

Eiden's hands dropped to his sides and he looked at his feet. He took a deep breath.

"Has anybody seen Jerry?" He looked up and glanced at Debbi and I.

"Jerry is here?" Debbi said, leaning forward. A guilty expression crossed her face and she bit her lip.

"We arrived together, tried to make a plan...but that man lives only in his head. He split as soon as we arrived. Mumbling something about the vents in the rear of the building. I came in the front door."

Debbi chuckled and her expression softened.

"That sounds like Jerry," she said. "But no, I haven't seen him."

"There is a black SUV around the East corner with a cell phone between the driver's seat and the armrest. Call the first number in the contact list then take the car and go wherever they tell you," Eiden said to Debbi.

Debbi nodded.

I hadn't known her long, but she didn't look like the lady who was afraid of losing her job.

She looked like a superhero.

"Good luck," Eiden said to Debbi. He brushed my shoulder with his knuckles. "Kid, you sure you're ready?

"Yes, sir," I said, hoping I sounded confident.

I hugged Debbi and we both followed Eiden to the hallway.

Two steps in and Eiden stopped, putting his hands behind his back.

I froze and held my breath.

A guy turned the corner from an open doorway right into Eiden's fist. He fell to the floor and didn't move.

I heard Debbi gulp and I wondered if she heard me finally start to breathe.

Eiden motioned for us to follow him again and we stepped quietly after him. I felt the cold press against my face and my ankles and saw snow gathering in the corners by the front door.

Eiden stopped and pointed his arm out towards a short hallway and looked at Debbi.

Debbi glanced at me and took a deep breath.

She ran hard. Her coat bouncing, arms pumping like she meant to outrun the whole building.

I didn't see her reach the door. Eiden grabbed my sleeve and we ran through the door with the stairs.

Eiden stopped and I ran into his back. I saw his shoulders tighten and his arm come back over my head. I ducked into the corner as a man dove into Eiden and they fell into the wall.

The fighting wasn't like the movies. It was loud and messy and too close to me. Boots scraped. Someone grunted. Eiden's shoulder hit the wall and the other man made a choking sound. I couldn't tell who was winning. The guy tipped backwards over me and I scrambled to the bottom step. It all blurred together until silence settled around me.

I closed my eyes and plugged my ears. Someone grabbed my knee and I jerked up. Eiden stood over me, pointing up the stairs, panting.

I stared at him and he reached out and squeezed my shoulder, almost like an apology.

We reached the final landing of the stairs and Eiden pushed me to the corner. He told me to wait then reached for the door.

The door swung open and the man in the white coat walked through, stopping so fast he nearly tipped forward.

After a beat, he glanced behind him and stepped onto the landing, shutting the door behind him with a thud.

"End of hall," he said, then ducked his head and rushed down the stairs.

I expected Eiden to chase him, but Eiden cracked his neck and opened the door.

I glanced over the railing at the floor below and saw the white coat jump off the last three steps and run through to the hallway.

Angry voices echoed from the hallway and bounced through the stairwell.

Hannah. I know that voice. She's in trouble!

"Hannah!" I said, running towards where it seemed her voice was coming from.

"Lincoln—wait!" Eiden said, rushing after me.

I ran straight for the door with a crooked number two and shoved it open.

CHAPTER FORTY

HANNAH

"YOU DON'T UNDERSTAND the position I was in," Harold said, his voice a mixture of defeat and frustration.

"I understand perfectly. You chose yourself," I shot back.

"I did what I—" Harold said.

The door by him exploded inward and a small body collided with my ribs so hard it knocked the air out of my lungs.

"Hannah!"

"Lincoln!" I squeezed him back as hard as he held me.

Eiden flew through the door whispering loudly. He saw me and stopped mid-sentence.

My shoulders dropped.

"Hi," I said, my voice breaking.

I was surprised by how much relief I felt.

"Hi," he answered.

"You," Harold said, breaking the moment. His voice cut through the room.

He stumbled toward Eiden like he was drunk. "You...fucked this up."

"Me? Why did you cancel the contract?" Eiden rounded his shoulders forward and took a half step closer to Lincoln and me.

Lincoln turned around and I wondered if he knew who the raving man in front of us was.

"You endangered everything! Why are you still watching Lincoln?!" Harold said.

"She wasn't," Eiden flung a finger at Renee then dropped it. "You weren't. Why shouldn't I?"

"Because now it's all a mess!"

"So you'd have rather your nephew die in that intersection?!" Eiden threw his hands up in the air, his back now in front of me.

Harold didn't answer at first. He stared at Renee like she was a ghost, which she nearly was.

For one suspended second, I saw Eiden—alive.

Jerry, half-hidden behind our company's crate.

Renee, pale, but breathing—clearly on a fresh high.

Harold unraveling.

Lincoln, pressed against my stomach, holding tightly to my hands resting on his shoulders.

Eiden, cut and bruised, standing between Lincoln and I and any threat.

Feet planted. Broad shoulders squared. Not moving.

And me? I wasn't sure I was feeling anything anymore.

We've protected Lincoln this far, can we keep going?

"No, no, of course not," Harold said, bringing me back to present, almost like he was answering me.

"Mom?" Lincoln said, looking around Eiden.

He broke free from my hands and rushed over to Renee.

The whole time I'd been wondering about him seeing Harold. His mom had been so silent, I'd forgotten she laid within reach.

Lincoln gently brushed a strand of frizzy hair off her forehead and straightened her blankets. Renee mumbled something and he leaned in.

"Yes, mom. It's me. I'm here."

Harold's mouth hung open watching Lincoln tenderly care for his mother. In his rage, he clearly hadn't realized Lincoln was here.

"You've gotten so big," Harold said, barely above a whisper.

"Are you Hannah's boss?" Lincoln said, glancing up at Harold.

Harold looked sad, then angry, then sad again.

His confused gaze found mine. His eyes asked me permission. Wondering if he should lie or be honest.

I nodded, hoping I read him correctly.

Harold took a deep breath. "I'm your uncle, Lincoln. I'm the one that's messed this whole thing up."

Harold deflated. Like someone had opened a valve in his chest and let the air out.

I smiled a little bit. Finally...honesty.

But what good does it do at this point?

"I thought I could manage both sides. I believed I was smarter than them," he said, watching Lincoln. "I partied too hard. I let a friend die." His voice cracked. "Your mom helped me move the body.

We didn't know his family was part of a gang. They found out and blackmailed me. Said they'd let me live if I shipped things for them. I played along. I didn't think they knew about Renee's part in it. So I hired someone to watch her. And then she started using. I didn't even know at first. Then she told me someone had given her something that helped her sleep. She wasn't built for this level of guilt...I guess none of us were. Never thought she'd be that person, though. My baby sister. What did I do to her?"

Harold had always been the "man in charge," the "big boss" at work. But right now, the broken man in front of me appeared younger than the nephew who stood before him, so forgiving.

"Two years ago, I went to the feds and told them almost everything. I wanted out. I dropped the private investigator. Then Leota showed up. He's my handler, my prison guard. I haven't been able to give the FBI anything since he showed up. They were too slow!" Harold looked behind him like he knew someone was listening.

"You tried to get rid of me!" Jerry said. "Why didn't you tell me you were working with the FBI?"

"Leota was watching. I was trying to protect you."

"I could have killed someone!"

I saw Jerry's fists ball up and his shoulders tense. Jerry moved before I understood what he was doing. His fist connected with Harold's cheek with a dull, ugly sound. Harold stumbled backwards and Lincoln rushed over.

"Ouch!" Jerry said, doubling over, grasping his fist.

I looked over at Eiden, expecting him to react, but he just smirked.

Harold righted himself and touched his cheek. He looked down at Lincoln.

"I'm a mess, kid," Harold said, looking at his blood-stained fingers.

Harold glanced at me helplessly.

Lincoln slipped his hand in Harold's. Shock flooded Harold's face. Lincoln tugged him closer to Renee and pressed his palm against hers.

“The doctor said Mom will be okay,” Lincoln said, studying Harold’s tear-streaked face. “But it’ll be hell for a while.”

The doorway darkened and dread knotted my stomach.

The man who showed us a hall pass stepped inside and stopped.

His eyes went first to Lincoln. Then to me. His jaw pulsed. I heard two hesitant clicks as he adjusted his grip on the gun.

“You were supposed to be gone by now,” he said.

Something almost human flickered across his face then his spine straightened and he moved to the side of the door.

Leota strolled in as if arriving late to an invitation-only party.

“Family meeting?” Leota drawled, rolling up his sleeve. “Makes clean-up so much easier.”

His dark eyes skimmed the room like he was counting bodies.

CHAPTER FORTY-ONE

HANNAH

"YOU REALLY THOUGHT you could outplay us, Harold?" Leota said. His voice rumbled my chest.

Lincoln dropped to the floor and crawled under the gurney. He covered his ears. His eyes were wide with fear. I wished he was still wrapped in my arms.

I wished I could transport him away from this trauma.

"It doesn't matter anymore," Harold said. His eyes flickered to Lincoln and back again. "I ruined her. I abandoned him. Just let them go. You have me."

I'd never seen Harold afraid before. His eyes tracked Leota like prey watching a hunter.

"Ha," Leota barked. "Your sister was so straight-laced, we worried she'd tattle. Took effort to soften her up. But once she learned she felt nothing, she begged for more. And we made sure she had it."

"You—drugged her? You?!"

Leota's sneer answered his question.

Harold roared and dove into Leota's stomach, knocking them both back into the wall. Leota shoved Harold off him and raised the gun.

Two shots rang out. Harold jerked back, his hands flying to his chest. He dropped to his knees, staring at Leota as if trying to memorize him, then collapsed.

I caught my breath and my ears rang. I reached for Eiden's hand in front of me and he held tightly. Jerry covered his mouth to suppress a scream.

"Anybody else?" Leota said, his gun level and ready. He ran his fingers through his hair and straightened his shirt. "This is how it's going to go. You," he pointed his gun at Lincoln and gestured toward me. "Go stand with them."

Lincoln crawled out from under the gurney and looked up at the ceiling as he walked over to me. I leaned down and picked him up. He wrapped his legs around me and buried his face in my neck, crying softly.

I wanted to tell him it would all be okay, but now, I didn't think it would be.

Eiden stood beside me. He put his arm around my shoulder and his other hand on Lincoln's back.

Jerry grasped and released his fists. His hands shook.

I looked up at Leota and saw sweat gathering at his temples.

The man behind him was staring at Harold, his gun lowered by his side.

I leaned my shoulder into Eiden's chest and he squeezed my shoulder, like he'd noticed, too.

Leota glanced behind him at the man and tilted his head towards us.

"Finish this," Leota said, and turned toward the door, holstering his gun.

"You've troubled this family enough," Eiden said, stepping in front of me. Lincoln tightened his grip on me.

Leota paused then turned around.

"What did you say?" He glared at Eiden.

"You asked for me. Here I am. You don't need them."

"You're such a white knight, aren't you?" Leota said pointing in the air as he listed the reasons he was annoyed. "Running to the FBI, interfering with our dosing, sacrificing yourself in such a heroic way."

Jerry stepped forward and clasped his hands behind his back.

"It was me. I told the feds." He looked down at the floor then over Leota's shoulder.

I wanted to whimper, to argue.

Leota pulled his gun out and tilted it towards Jerry.

Why wasn't Eiden moving? I wanted to scream. I was crushing Lincoln in my arms, wondering if I should turn around to protect him with my body. And would it even do any good?

But I felt the need to be silent. To be still. To wait.

Leota laughed. "Yeah, right. You wouldn't have the balls. You can't even look at me."

"No, really, it was me."

"Alright, then, you die." Leota cocked his gun. "And we'll make sure the FBI thinks you fled and they'll find evidence you were lying."

"Now!" Eiden yelled. Jerry fell to the floor and Eiden jumped over him, his fist connecting with Leota's gun. A shot fired and Renee's body bounced on the gurney.

Jerry dove to Renee and ripped off the sheet covering her. He put two hands on her stomach and leaned into her.

The man behind Leota moved suddenly. Deliberately.

He stepped around the fight like he'd been preparing for this moment. His hand closed around Lincoln's arm.

"No!" I cried, stepping backwards, tightening my grasp on Lincoln's waist.

He wrenched Lincoln from my arms so violently my nails scraped across Lincoln's coat. I lunged for him.

The man caught my hair in his fingers and yanked my head back, forcing my eyes to his.

The room froze.

His jaw flexed. His eyes did not waver.

He wanted me to trust him.

Lincoln screamed as my grip broke. I don't know if I let go, or if the man was stronger.

Then they were gone.

Eiden's fist connected with Leota's wrist. The gun skidded across the floor.

Leota pulled a knife and held it above his head, his shoulders squared. Eiden's hands came up, tracking the blade. He shifted his weight back, measuring distance.

I saw the blade flash and another shot cracked in the air.

Leota's head snapped sideways. He dropped to the floor, his collapse nearly as loud as the gunfire.

I reached out in front of me as if I was clawing for breath.

No one moved.

Silence settled into the room.

Then I saw Harold on the floor. A gun lay between his hands. Blood blooming across his shirt.

He smiled.

Then his eyes closed and his chest stilled.

Eiden stood over Leota and looked at me.

Leota was dead.

I stepped carefully to Harold and knelt next to him. I shook my head.

"Renee needs a doctor, now," Jerry called from the gurney.

I glanced from him to Eiden.

"Where did that man take Lincoln?"

CHAPTER FORTY-TWO

LINCOLN

HANNAH LET GO of me and I screamed. I didn't understand what was happening. There was too much noise. Too much movement. Then the man held me tight and told me he'd do what he could.

He'd held me before. He'd kept me warm.

I had to believe him, so I stopped fighting.

He carried me through the snow and shoved me into the front seat of a running car. He told me to buckle, and I did.

He drove fast but carefully, the snow swirling in ghostly patterns across the headlights. The man was talking. I'd never heard him speak above a whisper. He said he didn't like that kids were part of this, and he never agreed to it.

I got lost in his words. His voice was warm, like when he held me. He'd be good at reading bedtime stories.

I wondered about Uncle Harold. I'd seen him fall, but I didn't know if he was okay.

The car slowed after only a few minutes. He pulled over near a set of train tracks. Red lights blinked in the distance through heavy snow.

He pulled his winter hat off his head and settled it carefully onto mine, then told me to zip my jacket back up.

“Go to the tracks,” he said, gesturing forward but staring at the steering wheel. “Flag down the first car you see. Someone will stop.”

He looked over at me then. He didn’t look like a bad man with a gun anymore.

“I hope I can help more than this. But I can’t promise,” he said.

“You must go. Now.”

I opened the door and stepped into the cold air. My eyelashes were instantly coated with white flakes.

The engine roared to life and he was gone. The darkness settled around me as fast as the snowflakes buried my feet.

My fingers began to ache and I pulled them up inside my sleeves.

I could still hear Hannah screaming in my head, and I shivered.

I turned toward the blinking lights and started walking, trying to decide what I'd say if a car stopped.

CHAPTER FORTY-THREE

HANNAH

"I HAVE TO find him."

My voice didn't sound like mine. I felt frantic, but my voice sounded calm.

"Go, Hannah. Get out and find help. I'll stay with Renee," Eiden said taking over Jerry's medical aid by the gurney. Renee's eyelids flickered and she mumbled her son's name.

I carefully stepped around Leota's body and grabbed Renee's hand.

"We've got you, you're safe. You're going to be okay," I choked out. "I'll find Lincoln." Renee's fingers twitched and I knew she heard me.

Jerry pulled me from Renee's side and through the room. I looked back at Eiden.

"You can do this, Hannah," he said with a nod and a grim smile.

The hallways were abandoned and silent. Our footsteps echoed but we didn't care. Jerry and I ran down the stairs and to the front door, passing the small room that was once my prison.

Stepping out the door, my face was pelted with ice wind and heavy snowflakes. Everything was white, except one black SUV. The front door was open and the engine running.

I looked up at the building behind me and thought of all those who died today.

Harold's last stand.

Leota's bragging.

Eiden still protecting Lincoln.

A curtain on the third floor pulled back. The man who grabbed Lincoln from my arms stood backlit. He pointed at the running SUV, then disappeared.

I looked at Jerry.

"We can't trust him," Jerry said, staring at the running vehicle. A gust of wind wrapped around us and I stepped into the warm SUV.

"We don't have a choice," I said. "Get in. We can drive to the police station and get an ambulance for Renee."

I shifted into drive when I noticed a destination was set on the dash.

"Jerry! Maybe this is where Lincoln is! The police station is on the way. I'll drop you off and then follow the GPS."

For the first time in two days, I felt hope spread across my chest.

Four wheel drive kicked in immediately and I crept through the parking lot back onto the main road. Jerry grabbed the handle above his head as I skidded into a left turn. I hadn't driven a car in two years. And I would never intentionally drive in this weather.

The normally four minute drive to the station took a grueling eleven minutes because of the weather. I put the car in park in front of the police station. It sat across the street from where Ben read Jerry's note for me. I almost joked about how we thought his envelope might contain anthrax.

"You sure you're going to be okay? Why don't we get an officer first?"

"No time. If he's outside, he'll freeze. It can't get worse than this," I said.

Jerry nodded and shuffled to the front door, grasping tightly to the railing on the stairs.

I pictured Harold's bleeding chest, and Leota's exposed skull.

One more mile.

I realized the heater was still on high and I was sweating. I tried to stop at a red light but the SUV rolled through the intersection. My hands weren't shaking and I knew I was only focused on finding Lincoln.

I tapped the steering wheel as I slid through another intersection then turned right into a parking lot. The GPS said to go to the backside of an old train station building.

Today was my birthday. I'd forgotten until now.

Twenty-one, driving toward an unknown location on a GPS in a stolen car.

The wind was pushing snow across the parking lot. I knew Niawanda River was only a few steps away from the edge of the parking lot, but I couldn't see anything beyond my headlights.

I don't even know what I'm looking for.

I rounded the corner of the aged building and stepped on the brakes.

Lincoln was standing there; his arms wrapped around his body.

He stood under blinking track lights, snow catching on a hat slipping onto his eyes.

He looked smaller than the night we met.

Or maybe I just now understood how small he'd always been.

I stepped out of the car, and held on to the door, like I'd disappear with the wind.

He looked at me and adjusted his hat.

Three steps closer and he realized it was me. He trampled through the snow and fell into my arms. The wind swirled around us as I held him so tight he made a noise.

"It's over, Lincoln," I whispered.

"It's over."

EPILOGUE

HANNAH

THE FALL SUN was warm on my face. Aunt Viv said she'd stay at the lake house a few extra days before Milton dragged her back to Florida for the winter. Juliet purred in my lap as I watched Eiden secure a loose board to a new piece of plywood on the wooden porch.

"You wouldn't last a week," Ben said in a lighthearted tone.

"I would, too! Eiden," Lucy said. She stepped up on the porch and put her hands on her hips. "Does your PI office need a tech guru?"

"More like a tech nerd," Ben said. He stooped down to steady a board as Eiden secured another.

Eiden wiped his brow and glanced at Lucy. "I can put you in touch with my boss, Charlie."

"I'd like that," Lucy said, glancing down at her phone.

"Jerry can't make it," Debbi said, walking onto the back porch. She was followed by a heavy set, smiling man, their hands entangled. Debbi glanced back at him and grinned.

"He said lake houses are inefficient social structures," Lucy shrugged. "But he asked for pictures."

"You see the news on the sentencing?" I asked.

"Hard to miss," Eiden replied. "Can't believe it took eight months for them to finally pull the last string on that gang."

"Hannah!" Lincoln yelled. He dropped to the sand and covered his head. A water balloon soared over his back and popped beside him. "Missed!" He called over his shoulder to Renee.

Lincoln squealed as Renee grabbed his ankle and tripped him. She tackled him into the sandy beach, her melodic laugh a peaceful addition to the gentle breeze drifting off Lake Erie.

I stepped onto the sand and flexed my toes. I listened to the waves.

"I'll get you!" He giggled as he chased Renee to the water's edge.

"She starts back in the office tomorrow. Debbi and Renee made it through a lot," Eiden said, wrapping his arm around my shoulder.

"I wonder what happened to the not so evil bad guy," I said. "He wasn't part of any of the news stories."

Eiden nodded and rested his head against mine.

Lincoln dipped his toes in the water and splashed his mother. Her eyes were bright and her skin tanned.

Lincoln looked back at me and waved.

I smiled and waved.

This time, I didn't have to save him.

Some moments change you forever.

And others just teach you who you already were.

THANK YOU FOR READING MY NOVEL

I APPRECIATE YOU

OTHER THINGS I'VE DONE

Heart Pins (A Thriller)

Emotional Humidity: A Poetry Collection

Calvin and Ruby Play a Game (An Early Reader)

Calvin and Ruby Go to the Park (An Early Reader)

Calvin and Ruby Play Music (An Early Reader)

Calvin and Ruby Plant a Garden (An Early Reader)

UPCOMING THRILLERS

I Ain't This Brave for No Reason

Pawning Grudges

www.ingramcontent.com/pod-product-compliance
Lightning Source LLC
LaVergne TN
LVHW090545110826
845146LV00001B/27

9798995554004